My birthday was ruined.

"I don't believe it!" Lizzie shouted. "Did I just hear you invite Victoria Chubb to your birthday party?"

"She made me," I said weakly. "I don't know exactly how, but she made me invite her."

Lizzie scowled. "How could she make you?"

"You know how," I said sharply. "The same way she made us do the Creative Social Studies Project. It wasn't really my fault."

"Maybe your mother won't let her come," Lizzie suggested.

But my mother was no help. "If you've already invited her, you can't very well take back the invitation," she said. "But don't invite anyone else. Four friends are enough."

My birthday was ruined all because I couldn't keep my mouth shut. "I'm not having four friends at my party," I grumbled. "I'm having three friends — and one Victoria Chubb."

Other Apple Paperbacks you will enjoy:

Eat Your Heart Out, Victoria Chubb
by Joyce Hunt

My Sister, the Meanie
by Candice F. Ransom

Millicent the Magnificent
by Candice F. Ransom

The Four Of Us And Victoria Chubb

Joyce Hunt

AN
APPLE
PAPERBACK

SCHOLASTIC INC.
New York Toronto London Auckland Sydney

ISBN 0-590-42976-0

Copyright © 1990 by Joyce Hunt. All rights reserved. Published by Scholastic Inc. APPLE PAPERBACKS is a registered trademark of Scholastic Inc.

12 11 10 9 8 7 6 5 4 3 2 1   0 1 2 3 4 5/9

Printed in the U.S.A.   40

First Scholastic printing, August 1990

*For Martin Sacchetti, a wonderful critic
and a very special friend.*

1

"What do you think, Mom? The yellow blouse with the blue pants or the white skirt with the red T-shirt?" I stood in the kitchen doorway displaying both outfits impatiently.

My mother frowned and turned her attention from my brother, Lester Winchell II, who was gulping down his breakfast bottle. "I think whatever you decide to wear, it'd better be fast, Gina," she said. "The bus will be here at seven thirty-five."

"The bus is always late the first day of school," I said. But I knew she was right. It was seven-fifteen already and I still hadn't decided what flavor lip gloss to wear or whether to push my short hair behind my ears with or without bangs. Making important decisions always takes me a long time.

"However if it were me, I think I'd wear the white skirt with the red T-shirt," my mother said. "You see, Gina, there are problems with having too many clothes. It's hard to choose what to wear every day."

"That's *one* problem I love," I said, as I hurried off to my room. I had finally decided to try the yellow blouse with the white skirt.

Even though my mother is forever teasing me about my love of clothes, beauty aids like lip gloss and shampoo, and what she describes as my "amazing array of accessories," which includes a drawer full of scarves and jewelry, I know she enjoys clothes as much as I do. In the "old days," as my mother calls the time before the birth of Lester, my mom was a hostess at Chez Aperitif, one of the fanciest restaurants in town. Some of my best ideas for outfits have come from seeing how she used to dress for work.

"That orange scarf looks perfect against the yellow blouse," she told me a few minutes later, giving me a quick hug while I accepted a milky smooch from Lester. "Have fun!" she called as I headed for the bus stop.

As I hurried to the corner I couldn't help but think how unbelievable it was that summer vacation was really over. It had gone so fast. But I guess that was because I was working. Even though I'm only twelve, I was a partner in a company! My three friends, Roger Gordon, Lizzie Tanner, Edward (Buck) Buckley, and I had run Aces, a luncheonette that catered to kids. Actually, we'd done a pretty good job of it. In addition to solving a few problems that arose, we'd had fun and made a profit as well. We'd learned a lot about running a business and we'd sure learned a lot about people, too.

In the distance I spotted the boxy yellow school bus slowly rounding the corner. If things went the same as last year, my friend Lizzie was already aboard and had saved me a seat. Lizzie and I have been riding the school bus together since kindergarten. Sure enough, as I stepped on I saw Lizzie, waving from a seat near the middle.

"Neat outfit," she said as I slipped into the seat beside her. Lizzie had on jeans and a pink *Way to go, Cape Cod!* T-shirt. Her long brown hair was pulled into its usual ponytail, her sneakers a little scruffy on the toes. Lizzie isn't really into clothes the way I am. But she appreciates good taste. "I talked to Roger last night," Lizzie told me as the bus lurched away from my corner. "He and Buck aren't on this bus route anymore. They said to meet them in front of the gym to compare schedules."

"I hope we've got some classes together," I said, pulling my schedule from my purse to compare it with Lizzie's. They were totally different. And that was disappointing because over the summer, Lizzie, Roger, Buck, and I, who'd been pretty good friends since starting school, had gotten even closer. We'd learned that the four of us work well together — whether or not it was dealing with angry customers, or trying to figure out what to do about Victoria Chubb, a girl in our grade who caused us some anxious moments with the luncheonette. We always seemed to be able to come up with good solutions. I was hoping we could get together during the school year and do the same with homework assignments.

"I saw Victoria Chubb at the drugstore last night," Lizzie told me as the bus slowed down to make another pickup. "She was there buying last-minute notebooks and Hi-liters just like me."

"Lucky you," I said. Victoria Chubb is not exactly one of my favorite people. Although she has her good points, you can forget them quickly when she starts bossing you around or acting like a complete know-it-all and a total snob.

"How is she?" I asked Lizzie.

"Pretty much the same," Lizzie said. Then she frowned. "But she seemed awfully glad to see me. Something about her made me suspicious. And she kept saying she couldn't wait to see all of us back at school."

I understood what Lizzie meant. When Victoria Chubb seems glad to see you there probably is a reason to be suspicious. But right now there wasn't time to worry about Victoria Chubb. The school bus was pulling up to the school and kids were starting to unload. And on the very first day of school I figured, what could Victoria Chubb possibly do to bother us?

4

*   *   *

Once inside school Lizzie and I headed down the hall toward the gym. As we approached I could see Roger, who'd had a major growth spurt over the summer, towering over the water fountain. His brown hair was slicked back and he looked even taller than the last time I'd seen him, which was only a couple of days ago. Next to him Buck was leaning over the fountain, filling his cheeks with water, bending his head back to swallow it and then diving in for another refill. "Buck is on a new diet," Roger informed us. "Water is the only thing he can have all he wants of."

"I am *not* on a diet," Buck said, pulling his round face from the water fountain. "*My mother* is on a diet — and to make everyone in the house miserable she's accusing us all of being overweight." He patted his ample stomach. "I'm just a growing boy," he said.

Before any of us could comment the warning bell rang. Three minutes until first period. "What do you have first?" I asked Roger.

"Gym with Mr. Williams. What do you have?"

"Science with The Bug," I said, referring to Ms. Bugenhagen, everyone's favorite science teacher.

"I've got English with Ms. Delraney," Lizzie groaned. "I've heard she is an absolute witch and if every comma isn't perfect you fail automatically."

"I've heard the same thing," Buck said. "But

5

guess what?" he asked, studying his own schedule. "I'm in your class. At least you won't have to enter her torture chamber alone, Lizzie."

"Doesn't anybody have anything the same as me?" I wailed. Lincoln School is a pretty big place, but usually one of my friends is in a class with me.

"Doesn't look that way," Roger said, giving my schedule a quick glance. "I've got science fourth period with Buck. But other than that I'm on my own."

"Meet you at lunch," Lizzie said, starting up the hall. "Come on, Buck," she called. "Ms. Delraney takes off for being late, too."

Buck and Lizzie disappeared into the mass of students heading to classes on the first floor, Roger ducked into the gym, and I started for Ms. Bugenhagen's room, which was on the second floor.

Ms. Bugenhagen is one of the best science teachers in the whole school. Her classroom is always full of living things: plants, animals, and insects that she and her husband, who teaches biology at a college, spend their free time collecting. Ms. Bugenhagen wants her students to feel like real scientists when they are in her class. So even though most of the time she's not doing actual experiments, she always wears a white lab coat and carries a clipboard. Today, after she took attendance and passed out our books, she began

6

telling us what we were going to be doing in her class.

"Each of you will be responsible for three projects this semester," she told us. "The first project can be on any topic of your choice from the book. The second will be on a topic of my choice. And the third will be an independent research project." Ms. Bugenhagen rubbed her hands together. Her narrow brown eyes glittered. I could tell the independent research project was the one she was most interested in.

"Some time in the near future I will be giving each of you several seeds and directions for planting them. Your job will be to grow the seeds at home. As soon as you can identify what you've grown, bring your plant to school with a two-page report telling what it is and what it's used for."

A loud moan came from a bunch of boys at the back of the room. "What if our plants die before we can tell what they are?" one of them asked.

"It will be up to you to nurture the seedlings in such a way that they do not die before they can be correctly identified," Ms. Bugenhagen explained crisply.

"I have the world's biggest purple thumb," complained Cindy Lambert, a girl I knew from Girl Scouts a few years ago. I remember Cindy complaining when she had to sell cookies, too.

Ms. Bugenhagen was about to respond when a voice from the P.A. interrupted. "Ms. Bugenhagen, will you please send Gina Lazzaro to room 102? She is scheduled for a special meeting there."

Ms. Bugenhagen looked quizzically at me. I quickly picked up my books. Special meeting? What special meeting, I wondered?

"Read the first five pages of the text tonight, Gina," Ms. Bugenhagen told me as I left. "And be looking for ideas for your first project."

The door closed behind me and for a second I felt very lucky. It wasn't easy to get pulled out of a class at Lincoln School. And it wasn't too typical to be called to a special meeting either. For a second it occurred to me that it could be a mistake. Maybe some other Gina was supposed to be going to this meeting. But as I headed for 102 I decided it didn't matter. I already felt I needed a little change. For even though it was only the first day of school, I was starting to feel as if I'd never been gone for the summer.

As I started down the first floor hall toward room 102 I remembered that it was the small classroom the newspaper staff had used as their office last year. Could I somehow have gotten put on the newspaper this year? I wondered as I approached it. Ahead of me a teacher turned and pushed open the door to 102. I recognized him as Mr. Dale, one of the social studies teachers. I've never had Mr. Dale. And actually, I was glad, because I'd heard he was a little crazy. Mr. Dale was young and had a lot of new ideas when it came to teaching social studies. Seeing him now reminded me of a poster I'd seen around school last year. On it was a picture of Mr. Dale, dressed like a Marine, pointing his finger straight ahead. A caption under the picture read: WE'RE LOOKING FOR A FEW GOOD KIDS. I had never bothered to read why he was looking for those few good kids, and as I pushed open the classroom door I wondered if he was looking for them to be on the newspaper.

Inside was a long table. About a dozen kids were sitting around it. For a second I didn't see anyone I knew. Then suddenly I heard someone call "Gina!" It was Lizzie. She was sitting at the far end of the table next to Buck, who was sitting next to Roger.

"Lizzie, what are you guys doing here?" I called, hurrying over to an empty seat next to her.

"Who knows?" Lizzie whispered. "Buck and I are so glad to escape from Ms. Delraney's clutches we don't care what we're doing here."

"She wants us to do interpretive poetry readings in front of the whole class," Buck moaned.

"Forget the poetry, Buck," Roger said. "I want to know what we're doing here, too. I got pulled out of gym right in the middle of a volleyball game. And my team was winning!"

9

"I have no idea," Buck said, giving a loud snap to a piece of gum he was chewing. "But I'm not complaining."

At that moment Mr. Dale stood up. A big smile broke out beneath his bushy mustache as he cleared his throat for attention. Mr. Dale has long stringy hair that hangs down almost to his shoulders. He tucked a stray strand behind his ear and gazed at us all for a moment. Then he spoke in a deep enthusiastic voice.

"I am sure you can't know how happy I am to welcome you all to my Creative Social Studies Project," he began. "When those posters went up last year I was a little nervous, I'll confess. I was looking for a few good kids and, I can tell by the eager looks on your faces, that's just what I've got."

I looked at Lizzie and frowned. She shrugged her shoulders and passed the puzzled look to Roger. He returned it by rolling his eyes and nudging Buck. Buck looked at us all in complete confusion and I knew he must be thinking the same thing I was. For I was totally baffled. Somehow it appeared I had signed up for Mr. Dale's Creative Social Studies Project. But when had I done that? All the other kids in the room seemed to know what was going on. But the four of us were misfits. I was sure none of us had signed up for this project, yet somehow we were all here. Well, if somebody didn't speak up soon, I was going to raise my hand and tell Mr. Dale it was all a big mistake. I didn't need any more projects this semester, not with all Ms. Bugenhagen had planned.

"As you know," Mr. Dale went on, "each team of four is headed by a group leader." He stopped as the door to 102 suddenly burst open. "Ah, here comes one of the leaders now," he said with a pleased expression.

It was then that some of my confusion disappeared. Standing in the doorway, with a little smile and a glimmer I'd seen before in her small dark eyes, was our old friend, Victoria Chubb.

2

Although there is a lot about Victoria Chubb I don't like, one thing I have always liked is her style. Victoria's family has a lot of money. And they let Victoria help spend it. So her clothes are always different. You can tell Victoria shops at boutiques, not at the mall stores where I get most of my things. That's why I always try to make my outfits look different. When you shop at the malls you know there's going to be a good chance someone you know will show up with the same thing on.

Today there was no chance anyone in Lincoln School would show up in what Victoria Chubb had on. Her pants looked like they were made of an expensive linen my mother once pointed out to me in a fabric store. They were a creamy-peach color and she had on a fluffy, matching peach sweater. Around her neck were two thin gold chains. I don't know gold too well, but I would have bet this was the real stuff. It looked like an outfit even the teachers at our school wouldn't have been able to afford.

Victoria smiled sweetly at Mr. Dale. Beneath two stray curls that fell onto her forehead, her small dark eyes were quickly taking in the scene. She sat down in the front row and turned to smile sweetly at Buck, Lizzie, Roger, and me. None of us smiled back.

"Now we can proceed," Mr. Dale said jovially. "Each group is going to meet with its leader. You'll be getting your assignments, discussing any possible conflicts, and I'll be here to act as advisor if I'm needed. Remember, this is *your* project. For the next ten weeks you and your leader will be responsible for tackling some important community issues. Good luck!"

Although no one had said so, I was pretty sure who our leader was. And I was beginning to figure out how this whole situation had come about. My guess was Victoria Chubb had signed us up. Who else would have the nerve? Besides, after the summer with Aces, where the four of us were partners and Victoria worked for us, it made perfect sense to me that now she'd want a chance to be the boss. Well, if she thought I was going to spend the next ten weeks working for her, she had a shock coming.

As Mr. Dale stepped back and handed the meeting over to the leaders, three students stood up. One was Henry Richter, a brain since first grade, who was forever bringing in special projects on magnets, volcanoes, and foreign countries. Another was Tammi Chen, a cute, quiet girl whose family ran the computer store in town. Tammi was new to the school last year and I didn't know her too well. And the third was Victoria Chubb.

Tammi took a piece of paper from her notebook. "For my team," she said softly, "I have your assignments here." Three guys and a girl moved toward Tammi.

Henry Richter held up a thick notebook. "My plans are organized alphabetically," he announced. Mr. Dale nodded approvingly. "Spencer, Talbot, Weiss, and Zacarro are on my team." Kathy Spencer and Laura Talbot moved their chairs to join Julie Weiss and Bob Zacarro around Henry.

That left the four of us and Victoria Chubb. For a second no one spoke. I just looked at Victoria with the coolest look I could muster. I knew Buck, Roger, and Lizzie were doing the same.

Victoria came toward us with a big confident smile. At that moment, Tammi called to Mr. Dale. Victoria's smile quickly turned serious as Mr. Dale bent over to consult with Tammi.

"Isn't this a great idea?" Victoria said, gesturing us to follow her to the far corner of the small room. "I mean, I know you guys hate social studies just as much as I do," she continued in a hushed voice. "I almost failed it last year. My father was

14

furious with me. But I couldn't help it. All those confusing maps and globes. Who wants to read about the crops in other countries or how they get water for their toilets in the Middle East? I mean, is that boring or is that deadly boring?"

"Deadly boring," Buck said.

"But what's this?" Roger asked irritably. "I got pulled out of a volleyball game, Victoria. This better be good."

"Oh, it's good," Victoria said, giving Roger a little pat on the arm. "You know me. I wouldn't get you guys into something unless it was good. And it's going to be easy to get a good grade, too — I'm sure of that. If I get an A my father's taking me with him on his business trip to England. I'll get to see Buckingham Palace and the Queen. I'll get to ride on those neat double-decker busses and eat fish-and-chips outside. Now that's what I call real social studies."

I gave Lizzie a disgusted look. She was shaking her head in disbelief. "You mean you actually had the gall to sign us up for this course without asking our permission just to be sure you got an A so you could go to England with your father?!" she hissed at Victoria in a loud voice.

"Shh!" Victoria said, giving Mr. Dale's bent head a worried look. "When you hear what we get to do you'll thank me."

"So what do we get to do?" Roger asked.

"First of all," Victoria said. "We're excused

from regular social studies class two days a week. That means we're excused from half the papers that are due." She paused to let this sink in.

"That I like," Buck said.

"But what do we do on those two days?" Lizzie asked.

"We don't do book work," Victoria said. "We don't look at longitude or latitude or listen to other kids' reports on how people live in the communist countries. What we do is activities. It's fun."

"*Activities?*" Roger asked. "What kind of 'fun activities'?" I could tell that Roger was not happy about being pulled out of gym class by Victoria Chubb. I knew from the summer that he didn't trust Victoria, and unlike Buck, who could be talked into anything if fun or food were mentioned, Roger was not about to be convinced easily.

"Here," Victoria said, pulling out a chair. "Let's sit here at the end of the table and discuss this." As the four of us sat down, Victoria remained standing. "As Mr. Dale said," she began, "the Creative Social Studies Class is composed of teams. There are four people on each team and one leader. I'm the leader of your team."

"Naturally," Lizzie said sarcastically.

"Look, Victoria," I said. "You had a lot of nerve signing us up without asking us. I don't think I even want to do this, so don't go around telling people I'm on your team."

16

"Gina's right," Roger said. "What makes you think we want any part of these 'fun activities'?"

"I signed you up because I saw how well we worked together this summer," Victoria said. "Look at all the problems we solved working at Aces. And we're still friends."

Before anyone could dispute that, Mr. Dale strolled over. "How's it going on the Chubb Team?" he asked cheerfully.

"Absolutely great," Victoria replied. "I was just about to describe the assignments to my team members. I know they're going to be excited about all the good they'll be doing."

"Yes," Mr. Dale said dreamily. He gazed at us all with pride. "You have no idea the wonderful feeling you'll get when you've been out in the community, actually helping people who need the energy and spirit of the young people in this area. There's nothing like it."

At that moment I wanted to stand up and tell Mr. Dale the entire story. I wanted him to know that none of us had any intention of joining his Creative Social Studies Class, that we'd been forced into it by Victoria just so she could get an A and go to England, and that all we wanted to do was get out of it. But there was something about Mr. Dale that made it impossible to do this. Maybe it was the hopeful look in his eyes as he talked, or the fact that he seemed so sincerely enthusiastic about this project stuff that stopped me. But whatever it was, it worked. Like Buck, Roger, and Lizzie, I kept my mouth shut, and sat and listened as Victoria described our activities.

With a quick shake of her curly head, Victoria began. "Our team will be working with two third-graders. These girls need tutoring in reading, and because Lizzie is such a good reader, I've assigned that project to her," Victoria announced. She looked at Lizzie for approval. Lizzie just stared at her.

"I also have two blind women who would like to be read to. Gina has a lovely voice, so I'm going to let you do that," she told me.

"What do I have to read?" I asked. "And where is this all going to take place?"

"You can discuss what to read with them," Victoria told me. "The first session, which is tomorrow, is a planning session. You'll meet your people and decide what to do. And it's all going on here at school. Mr. Dale will be picking up the participants in his van."

"What have I got to do?" Buck asked.

"Your project is slightly different," Victoria told him. "But I know you'll like it. There's an elderly couple who live up the street from school. They're housebound, so you'll be asked to do errands for them. You know, pick up things at the drugstore, mail letters, get them some groceries."

Just the suggestion of food seemed to please

18

Buck. "Sounds good to me," he said with an easy nod.

"And Roger, I know how you like gym," Victoria went on. "There's a group of nine-year-old boys who need a basketball coach. I think you'll be perfect for that assignment."

Roger shrugged his shoulders and mumbled, "Yea, sure," under his breath. But even *he* didn't seem as opposed to the idea as he had been a few minutes ago. And I could see why. It was pretty interesting. And it was certainly different from the social studies we were used to.

"So, what do you think?" Victoria asked eagerly. "Is this a great idea or what?"

"It is pretty neat," Buck said. "I mean, we're out of class, we get to do things instead of writing all the time. . . ."

"And what do you do, Victoria?" Lizzie asked. "What's your project?"

"The leaders are responsible for organizing everything," Victoria said. "I have to hand in a detailed report of how everything goes. And of course, if you have any problems at all you come to me and I solve them for you." She paused and her bright little eyes flashed at us. "So what does everyone say?"

I know what Victoria expected us to say. She expected us to say, *Great, we'll do it. Whatever you say, Victoria, we're here to serve you.*

And the thing is, I was about ready to say that. After all, it did sound like it could be fun. Luckily Roger wasn't so easy to convince.

"I don't know about anyone else," he said. "But I have to think this over. I didn't sign up for this project and I'm not sure I want to do it."

"But you have to," Victoria said, and I could hear the desperation in her voice. She must really want that trip badly, I thought. "Come on," she pleaded. "I already told Mr. Dale."

"That's your problem," Roger said. He looked at Lizzie, Buck, and me. "I'm going back to gym class right now but if you guys want, we can meet at my house after school and talk this over."

"But . . . " Victoria began again.

"You can't make us do it, Victoria," Lizzie said, standing up. "All we have to do is say we never signed up for it in the first place and you'll really fail social studies this year. We'll let you know our decision tomorrow."

"I agree with Lizzie and Roger," I said, pushing my chair back. "I've got to think this over."

"It sounds pretty good to me — " Buck began. Then he caught the looks Roger, Lizzie, and I were giving him. " — but I'll let you know to-morrow, too," he added weakly. "Maybe I'm miss-ing something."

The four of us walked out of room 102 together. As we did the bell for second period rang. "My house right after school," Roger reminded us. "And be thinking about what you really want to do. This isn't a five-person team, you know," he called as we all started off in different directions. "It's really the four of us versus Victoria Chubb."

3

I wasn't sure about Lizzie, Buck, and Roger, but the day passed, the more I thought about the Creative Social Studies Project the less it appealed to me. First of all, I don't know where Victoria got the idea that I had such a lovely voice, but it had never seemed that terrific to me. I have a regular old voice that sounds squeaky when I get nervous and flat when I'm just making conversation. It's nothing special, and thinking back I realized that Victoria probably just told me my voice was special to flatter me. My voice is no better and no worse than any other voice in Lincoln School.

Not only that, but I just couldn't picture myself reading to two blind women. I like to read aloud to myself — when I feel like it. But I didn't want to be forced to read two days a week some book I probably wouldn't even be interested in and feeling uncomfortable the whole time. Actually, nothing about the idea appealed to me, and by the time I got to Roger's that afternoon I had made up my mind: I was getting out of the Creative Social Studies Project the next day.

I could tell by the look on Roger's face as he opened the front door and peered down at me that he was feeling the same way. "Hi," he grumbled.

"Something smells good," I said, trying to sound cheerful. Since Roger's brother Tommy left for college last month, Roger hasn't been his usual sensible self. He idolizes Tommy and misses him being around the house, even though most of the time Tommy was working part-time delivering pizzas, or hanging out with his girlfriend.

"I'm making popcorn," Roger said. "Buck's here and he begged me to make some. With real butter, of course."

I followed Roger to the kitchen where Buck was holding a big wooden bowl under a hot-air popcorn popper that was spouting a steady stream of snowy popcorn. "The butter's melting, the popcorn's popping, and all's well in the world," Buck said happily.

"No it isn't," Roger muttered. "Not as long as I'm coaching those fourth-graders in basketball. I can't believe Victoria Chubb had the nerve to sign us up in the first place. And now she thinks she can tell us what we're going to do." Roger pulled out a chair and sat down glumly at the kitchen table. "Well, I'm not coaching a bunch of little kids in basketball. I don't even like basketball and I'm a horrible player. Besides, someone has to teach her a lesson. I think what she did was very selfish. Just because she wants to go on a trip across the ocean, why should we have to suffer?"

"I agree," I said, taking a handful of popcorn and sitting down at the kitchen table. "I don't want to spend two days a week reading stories to some blind women either. It's not that I don't want to help people," I explained. "But I want to do it when I want to do it — not just because Victoria Chubb doesn't like social studies and thinks she might fail."

The doorbell rang and Roger went to let Lizzie in. "What do you think, Buck?" I asked.

"I don't mind running errands," Buck said, delicately drizzling melted butter over the top of the popcorn. "I need the exercise and it will be fun to get out of school for a while."

"But doesn't it make you mad to think Victoria is bossing us around?" I asked. "And that she took it upon herself to assume we'd do this?"

"I guess so," Buck said. But I wasn't sure he meant it. He had sprinkled salt and a smattering of Parmesan cheese over the bowl of popcorn, and he was looking at it with such pleasure that I knew nothing short of having his lips stapled shut could bother him at this moment.

"Lizzie agrees with us," Roger announced, leading Lizzie into the kitchen.

"I don't feel like tutoring anyone this year,"

Lizzie complained, sinking into a chair next to me and reaching for the popcorn. "In fact, if I'm ever going to pass Ms. Delraney's class I'm going to have to be tutored myself. That woman is the pickiest thing alive. Do you know, she won't even let us use contractions when we write?"

"What are contractions?" Buck asked, digging into the bowl. "I don't think I'd even know how to use them."

"You just used two," Lizzie told him.

"Then I'm smarter than I think," Buck said, stuffing a handful of popcorn into his mouth. "Maybe I should do the tutoring."

"You can do the tutoring if you want," Lizzie said. And as she said it I realized maybe she was actually serious.

"Do you want to run the errands?" Buck asked her.

"Not really," Lizzie admitted. "That's the thing. I wouldn't mind doing something. But I don't want to tutor — and I'm not sure if it's because I don't want to *tutor*, or if it's really because I don't want to do what Victoria Chubb tells me to do."

"I know just what you mean," Roger said. "The whole idea isn't so bad. It's just that I hate to give Victoria the satisfaction of telling us what *she* thinks we should be doing. We know ourselves better than *she* does."

Lizzie's face had a troubled frown and I could tell the whole thing was really bothering her.

"You see, being involved in a project like this would look good on our school records," she admitted. Unlike the rest of us, Lizzie is already planning for college. Her dad is a lawyer, which is what Lizzie thinks she wants to be, and she actually knows which law schools are considered good and which aren't so good. Naturally she worries about getting into one of the good ones.

"And I *could* use the change," Roger conceded. "I still miss running Aces. But basketball isn't for me. If Victoria knew me at all she'd know that much."

"I don't mind basketball," Buck said.

"So do you want to coach the team?" Roger asked.

"Sure," Buck replied. "Needs more salt," he added, sprinkling a generous amount of salt over the popcorn.

"I thought you were going to do the tutoring," Lizzie told him.

"I'm not smart enough," Buck said.

"You just said you were smarter than you realized," I reminded him. But I was starting to get an idea. If we could each choose our own assignment, instead of being ordered around by Victoria Chubb, maybe this project wouldn't be so bad after all.

"I'm smart enough to coach basketball," Buck said. "But not to tutor."

"I suppose I could tutor," I said reluctantly, not

at all sure I truly meant it. In a way, I do like little kids. Besides, it would be good experience for when Lester gets to school. "But if I tutor, who's going to read to the blind women?" I asked.

"Not me," Roger said. "No basketball, no reading, and no tutoring for me."

"That leaves errands," I said. "Would you do the errands?"

"Yes," Roger said. "But that means Buck has to do the basketball and Lizzie the reading, right?"

"I read all the time anyway," Lizzie said. "I might as well read to someone else."

"The more I exercise the more I need to eat," Buck said. "So if I were coaching basketball I'd need to increase my calories on those days, right?"

"You'd probably have to double them," Roger said.

"I'll be glad to coach the basketball team," Buck told us. "Got any diet soda around, Roger?"

As Roger pulled open the refrigerator door, Lizzie quickly reviewed what we'd just decided. "So Roger will do the errands, Gina will do the tutoring, Buck is the coach, and I'm doing the reading. Is that right?" We all nodded.

"Except for one little thing," Roger said, bringing out a bottle of soda and placing it before Buck. "Our leader may not agree with these changes."

"She has to," I said. "Or else we quit."

"That's right," Lizzie said. "We have every right to choose our own assignments. If she

27

doesn't like it, we just tell her we're not doing anything."

"So who tells her?" Roger asked, getting four glasses from the cupboard. "We've got to tell her before tomorrow, so I'll volunteer the use of my phone. But I'm not calling."

"Me, either," Buck said.

"I can't believe you're afraid of Victoria Chubb," I told Buck.

"I'm not afraid of her," he said. "I just don't want her getting the wrong idea. If I called her up, she might think I liked her."

"He's right — she'd be telling everyone in school if Buck or I called her," Roger added, coming to Buck's defense. "Why don't you call her, Gina? Tell her what we've decided. Or are you afraid of her?"

While I am not actually afraid of Victoria Chubb, for some reason the thought of calling her made me nervous. Luckily for me, it didn't make Lizzie nervous at all.

"I'll call her," Lizzie volunteered. "Give me the phone book. We're right and she's wrong, so what can she say?" I knew then and there Lizzie would make a great lawyer.

She flipped through the phone book looking for Victoria's number. "Here it is," she said. "Arthur Chubb on Wintercrest Road." But even as Lizzie dialed, my stomach felt a little jumpy.

"May I please speak to Victoria?" Lizzie asked,

sounding confident and businesslike. She covered the receiver and whispered to us, "I think a maid answered. She's calling for Miss Victoria right now."

"Hello, Victoria? This is Lizzie Tanner. I just want to let you know . . ."

Then for a few moments Lizzie didn't speak. She frowned; she nodded; finally she shook her head. "Look, Victoria, I'm sure it is important to you to get an A in social studies. And if your father has promised to take you to England if you get an A, I'm sure that's important, too. But you still had no right signing us up for this project without asking us first!"

To my surprise Lizzie was actually almost yelling at Victoria. Roger was clapping his hands together silently urging her on, and Buck was nodding his support as he gulped down the soda. From the sound of the conversation, I didn't think we'd end up doing the social studies project at all. But, as usual, I had underestimated Victoria. For suddenly Lizzie fell silent.

"Mr. Ramstead?" I heard Lizzie say in a slightly lower tone of voice. "What's Mr. Ramstead got to do with this?"

Mr. Ramstead is the assistant principal. As he himself grimly describes his job, he is in charge of discipline and decorum at Lincoln School. Most kids would rather crawl into the cage of a hungry tiger than get called to Mr. Ramstead's office.

"You don't exactly understand, Victoria," Lizzie went on quickly. "I'm not calling to say we won't do it at all. I just want to tell you about a couple of changes we've made. You see, Buck would rather do the basketball, Gina wants to tutor, Roger will do the errands, and I'll do the reading. How's that sound?"

I frowned at Buck and Roger. It wasn't like Lizzie to back down. But now she was nodding enthusiastically as Victoria talked. "Great. See you tomorrow," I heard her say to Victoria before she hung up.

Lizzie looked at us sheepishly. "Well, it's all set," she said, trying to sound optimistic. "I mean, we did say we'd try it, didn't we?"

"What's Mr. Ramstead got to do with this?" Roger demanded.

Lizzie sighed. "According to Victoria, she had an interview with the local newspaper after school today. Mr. Ramstead was in charge of the whole thing. Victoria told them all about her team and what projects we'd be doing. Mr. Ramstead was very impressed. She said if we wanted to get out of it now, we'd have to go to him to explain. And the story is scheduled to run in this week's paper."

"But what if we explained that she signed us up without our permission?" Roger asked.

"She said it's too late now. We should have told Mr. Dale at the meeting today. And I'm afraid she's right," Lizzie said glumly.

"It's not that I mind doing it," I said. "Actually I like the idea of it. It's just getting pushed around by Victoria that I don't like. Why do you think she does these things?"

"Because she's spoiled," Roger declared, setting his empty glass down with a bang. "She always gets her own way at home and she thinks she can get it with other people, too."

"I don't know," Buck said. "I think part of it is that she wants to be included with our group. But if that's it, somebody ought to tell her she's going about it in all the wrong ways. How about it, Lizzie?" he teased. "Do you want to call her back and tell her that?"

Lizzie smiled. "No thanks," she said. "And when you think of it, how bad can this project be? After all, we'll be getting out of class, and it will look impressive on our records. And it is the four of us against Victoria. When you think of it that way, how bad can it be?"

No one had an answer and so we went on to finish up the popcorn. But as we later learned, none of us had an answer because at that time none of us could have imagined just how bad it could be.

4

The next morning I had an even harder time trying to figure out what to wear than I had the first day of school. It was the first day of the project, and if I was supposed to be tutoring I figured I should dress like a teacher. But what kind of teacher?

I thought about the teachers in our school. Ms. Bugenhagen certainly never had this problem. All she had to do was slip on a white lab coat every morning. Ms. Delraney was into suits, skirts, and blouses. Her outfits were always navy, gray, or brown, with white blouses and pretty pins at the neck. She dressed in the same fussy way she marked papers.

Then I thought of Ms. Cipperly and Mrs. O'Keefe. They were two of the younger teachers and they really seemed to like teaching. When you'd pass them in the hall they'd be laughing or joking about something. They both taught home ec and they liked to make their own clothes. Some of the outfits they made were really wonderful.

As I put together my outfit that morning I decided that if I had to dress like a teacher, I'd try to dress like Ms. Cipperly and Mrs. O'Keefe.

"That outfit is smashing," my mother said, as I stood in the kitchen a few minutes later gulping down a glass of orange juice and munching on an English muffin.

"Thanks," I said. Sometimes, when I put on different combinations of clothes, I'm not sure if they look good or not. A word of praise from my mother always helps me feel better and I know my mother doesn't use a word like *smashing* unless she really means it.

"You really think this is 'smashing'?" I asked her. I was wearing baggy pants in a wild cranberry, black, and green print with a cranberry blouse and a long green vest. Around my waist was a shimmery gold belt. I had decided to wear my black hightop sneakers so I wouldn't look too dressy.

"You're making a fashion statement," she told me, as Lester let out a wail from his high chair, indicating he knew I was getting attention and he wanted to be part of it. "You're showing the world you have good taste and daring." She glanced at the clock. "Now you better get moving or you'll miss the bus and no one will get to see your statement."

Lizzie liked my fashion statement. "Neat," she said as I slipped into the seat on the bus next to

33

her. "I wish I could put things together like you do. But they wouldn't look the same on me."

She patted a book she was holding on her lap. "My father let me borrow his thesaurus. Can you believe Ms. Delraney has us taking a quiz already? We have to choose a poem from three she's going to select, then explain it in our own words. So I have that to look forward to. And reading to those two women. Will I ever be glad when this day is over!"

"I know what you mean," I said. I felt a little tingle of anxiety in the bottom of my stomach. It seemed silly to be nervous about third-graders, but for some reason, I was. What if they didn't like me? What if they didn't want to learn what I was supposed to teach them? There were bound to be some difficulties. But the biggest one was, when those difficulties arose we had to take them to Victoria Chubb to be solved. I knew Lizzie felt the same way, and as the bus pulled up to the school, I felt, despite my great outfit, a funny sense of dread.

At one-thirty that afternoon the same group of kids that had met in room 102 the day before gathered there again. "Over here, Gina," Victoria called, waving to me as I entered.

Victoria was wearing a straight black skirt, a white blouse with lace on the collar, nylons, and flat black pumps. I couldn't help but think she looked ready for a funeral. She already had Lizzie and Buck in the same corner where we'd met yesterday.

"Now let me get this straight," she said, taking a legal pad out of a leather briefcase she was carrying. "Lizzie's reading, Buck's coaching, Roger's running errands, and Gina's tutoring, right?"

"That's right," I said.

Victoria frowned at me. I could see her eyes going up and down my body, from the tips of my black hightops to the green barrettes I'd put in my hair to hold back the bangs. "Since part of my responsibility is directing the people who are working for me, I have to tell you, Gina. I think your outfit is a little too flashy for tutoring."

For a second I couldn't speak. *Too flashy for tutoring!* Had I really heard those words? Who was Victoria Chubb to tell me how to dress? I could feel my cheeks begin to burn as I tried to think of what to say. No words came out.

It was Buck who spoke. "I think she looks neat," he said.

"I'm not saying she looks messy," Victoria said, purposely misunderstanding what he meant. "I'm just saying that we will be making an impact on younger students. As your leader it is my responsibility to help you do the best job you can . . ."

"How Gina or anybody else is dressed isn't going to make a bit of difference when it comes to the job they do," Lizzie interrupted. Her voice was sharp with anger. "If you don't like the way we look maybe you better get a new team!"

At that moment Roger ambled in, with Mr. Dale behind him. He'd just arrived from picking up the people we'd be working with from outside the school.

"This team is fine," Victoria said quickly. "I'll just ask Mr. Dale what he thinks," she said, jotting something down on her legal pad. "Maybe it doesn't matter after all."

"Everyone's here," Mr. Dale announced happily. "And they're all dying to meet you. So leaders, if you'll tell your teams where they're to report, we're ready to start the Creative Social Studies Project!"

I rolled my eyes at Lizzie. I couldn't help it. As much as I admired Mr. Dale's enthusiasm, I could not feel it myself. From the very start this project had problems. And as long as Victoria was in charge, I couldn't see how they were going to get any better.

I looked around. The other leaders were consulting their notes and kids were leaving room 102 for their assignments.

"Buck, you go to the gym," Victoria directed. "Lizzie, the women are in the library. Roger come with Mr. Dale and me to get directions. And Gina, you stay here. The tutoring is right here in 102."

I glanced at the door and sure enough, two little

girls were peering inside. They looked about eight years old and scared.

"Come on in, girls," Mr. Dale called to them. "Let's see, who's doing the tutoring?" he asked, consulting his list. "Gina Lazzaro. Good choice, Victoria."

Victoria smiled smugly at the compliment, apparently forgetting she'd originally had me doing the reading.

"Come here, girls," Mr. Dale said, as the two third-graders cautiously approached us. "This is Gina," Mr. Dale said. "She'll be working with you."

The two little girls looked up at me with wide, wary eyes. They each clutched two books, a notebook, and a crayon box. "This is Ellissa Stanton and this is Tracey Clarke," Mr. Dale told me. "They can't wait to get started, right girls?"

The two girls nodded silently. "I'll leave you three here to get to know each other," Mr. Dale said. "Roger, I need to give you directions. And leaders come with me. We'll discuss any difficulties you've noted so far."

I saw Victoria give me one final head-to-toe look as she followed Mr. Dale and the rest of the leaders from the room. The door closed and I turned to face Ellissa and Tracey.

"I'm Gina," I said. "Which one is Ellissa?"

The taller of the two girls, who had a thin

pointed face and thick black straight hair that hung down over her shoulders, said in a barely audible voice, "I am."

"And you must be Tracey," I said, smiling at the other girl, a tiny blonde with round green eyes. Tracey nodded silently and looked down at her books.

"Why don't you girls sit down at the table and we'll look through the books you have and find a nice story to read," I said, trying to give my voice a little enthusiasm. "Let's see," I said, leafing through one of the books, a reader I remembered from third grade. "What are some of the good stories in this book?"

"There aren't any good stories in that book. They're all bad stories," Tracey said. Ellissa giggled.

"There must be one good one that you like," I said.

"I like your pants," Tracey said. "I wish my mother would buy me a pair of pants just like yours. And a shirt and a vest like yours, too. All I get to wear are dopey overalls." She gave the strap of her denim overalls an impatient snap.

"Me, too," said Ellissa. "What color is that nail polish you've got on? It looks like the color the lady wore in *Murder Every Midnight*. Did you see that movie? My mother wouldn't let me stay up to watch it all. I have to go to bed at eight-thirty — even on weekends! My mother is so mean. She always makes me go to bed just as somebody is about to get killed in a movie but she lets my older brother stay up and watch. My mother is the meanest."

"*My* mother is the meanest," Tracey said. "She's meaner than your mother. She won't even let us rent videos if there's anybody getting killed in them. Don't you think that's mean?"

"When I was in third grade I couldn't watch that kind of movie either," I said. "But we're not here to talk about videos. We're here to read. Now pick a story." I tried to make my voice sound firm but it was hard. Wait until I told Victoria how the girls had liked my outfit. That would give her something to think about.

"I don't want to pick a story," Ellissa said.

"Me neither," Tracey said.

"Then I'll pick a story," I said. " 'The Rabbit and the Hound.' It's on page forty-six. Let's read that."

"I hate that story. It's dumb," Ellissa said. Her book remained closed on her lap.

"It's too hard," Tracey agreed. "I don't want to read that one. I hate hounds. They're mean, like my mother. She won't let me take tap dancing lessons either. Do you know how to tap dance, Gina?"

"No," I said. "But I do know how to read." I was starting to lose my patience. "If you don't want to read that story, then let's open to the first one. This looks good," I said, flipping back to page one. "It's about going to the fair."

"That story is too babyish," said Ellissa.

"Right," Tracey agreed. "My baby sister could read it. And she can't even read." She started to giggle. "Get it, Ellissa? That's how babyish that story is." Ellissa started to laugh.

"I'll read the first sentence," I said. "Tracey can read the second. And Ellissa can read the third." Somewhere I thought I could remember my mother saying if you ignored naughty behavior in little kids it would go away.

"That's too boring," Ellissa said. She opened her crayon box. "I have three barrettes," she said. "Will you put them in my hair the way you have those in your hair?"

"If I do, will you read with me?" I asked.

"Yes," Ellissa said, handing me the two barrettes. "Here," she said. "I have a comb in this crayon box, too. Make it look just like yours."

Carefully I combed her long black hair. Then I drew the bangs back, as I had done my own that morning, and held them down with the barrettes. "How does it look?" Ellissa demanded when I was done.

"Very nice," I said.

"Neat," Tracey said.

"I want to see. Do you have a mirror?"

"No," I said. "Now we have to read."

"I can't read until I see how I look," Ellissa

insisted. "Let's go to the bathroom and look in the mirror."

"After we read," I said. My voice was a little louder than it had been so far.

"I have to go to the bathroom now," Tracey whined. "I can't wait or I might have an accident."

"Gerry May had an accident in our class this year," Ellissa said. "His mother had to bring in new jeans for him. He was crying."

"If I take you to the bathroom will you come back here and read — and do nothing else?" I asked. I didn't want any accidents my first day of tutoring.

"Yes!" both girls said together.

"Promise?" I asked.

"Yes," they agreed.

We left room 102 and headed down the hall to the bathroom. While Tracey and Ellissa were in the stalls I fixed my hair and put on a little more root beer lip gloss. I straightened the collar of my blouse, retied my sneakers and washed my hands. "Come on, girls," I warned. "We're wasting valuable reading time."

"You should never rush people in the bathroom," Tracey called out to me. "My father says it's not healthy."

A few minutes later they both emerged. "I need more soap than that," Ellissa said, holding out her two hands so I could push out the foamy soap for her. "See," she said, putting a dab of soap on each

41

cheek. "I have whipped cream on my face."

"I want to do that, too," Tracey whined. "Give me some more soap."

"Look," I said. And now I wasn't pretending. I was really getting mad. "If you two don't cut out the fooling around and get back to the reading I'm going to tell Mr. Dale and he won't let you get out of school to come here anymore."

That seemed to work. Quietly Ellissa and Tracey followed me back to room 102. Without a word they sat down and picked up their books. "Now," I directed. "Turn to page one." Without any protest they did so. "Who can read the title of this story?"

Both girls sat mutely. I pointed to the first word of the title. "Who knows what this word is?" Both girls looked blankly at it. "No one knows this word?" They both shook their heads and I had the feeling they weren't just trying to get out of reading. I had the feeling they truly couldn't read the word. "Then I'll read the title," I said. "The name of the story is 'Adventure at the Fair.' It sounds exciting, doesn't it?"

Tracey shrugged. Ellissa made a face. "Well I think it sounds exciting," I said. "I can't wait to see what the adventure will be."

"A little kid gets lost and the elephant keeper finds him," Ellissa said.

"So you've already read the story?" I asked.

"The top reading group read it last year," Tracey told me. "I heard it then."

"We weren't supposed to listen but we couldn't help it," Ellissa explained. "The good readers like to read loud."

Suddenly, in spite of how hard Tracey and Ellissa were making my job, I felt a little sorry for them. I hadn't been in the top reading group in third grade either. And I could remember listening to all the stories before I got the chance to read them myself, because what Ellissa said was true. The good readers did like to read loud. Now I wondered if I should continue with 'Adventure at the Fair' or go on to something else that maybe they hadn't already heard.

Luckily I didn't have to make the decision, for just then the door opened and Victoria appeared. "Time's up," she said. "Mr. Dale needs everyone back at the van." She glanced at Ellissa and Tracey, who were sitting at the table with me, their reading books opened in front of them, and gave us all an approving nod. "Looks like you did a lot of reading today," Victoria said. Then she was gone.

I looked at Tracey and Ellissa. They looked back at me with wide, innocent eyes. And I knew we were all thinking the same thing. In fact, not one word had been read by either of the girls.

"This was fun," Ellissa said, giving her new

hairdo a proud pat and gathering up her things.

"And the van ride's fun, too," Tracey said. "We'll see you in two days," she added, as they started down the hall to the gym where they were to meet Mr. Dale.

Walking along I felt like a complete failure. How could I be expected to get these two girls interested in reading when all they wanted to do was talk about clothes and videos? And even if I did admit to Victoria Chubb that I was having problems (which I was not about to do), what could she do to help?

Just then I spotted Buck coming out of the gym. "Buck!" I cried. "How'd the basketball coaching go?"

One look at Buck's face told the entire story. His cheeks were as round and red as ripe apples, his eyes shiny with anger. "It was a horror story," he told me, as we walked out to our busses together. "I had six guys who spent most of the hour arguing with each other, fighting over who got the ball first, and paying no attention to the fact that they were supposed to be a team. I had to break up three fights and to make matters worse, the six guys only had three names."

"What?"

"Yep. Two Timmys, two Eddies, and two Peters. Do you know how confusing that can be when you're trying to yell at somebody?"

"So what are you going to do?" I asked. It

44

sounded like Buck's experience had been just about as terrible as mine.

"I don't know," he said. "How did the tutoring go?"

"It was awful," I replied. "The girls weren't interested in learning new words. All they wanted to do was get their hair done and tell me how mean their mothers are. To be perfectly honest, I feel more like quitting now than ever."

"Me, too," Buck said. He gazed at me for a second without speaking. But he didn't need to. I knew just what he was thinking.

"So why shouldn't we?" I asked. "We didn't sign up for this. And we've given it a chance. And we don't like it. Too bad for Victoria Chubb. Let her explain her way out of it."

"That's what I was about to say," Buck agreed, as he started for his bus. "I'm telling her first thing tomorrow. And you're right. Too bad for Victoria Chubb. If she hadn't opened her big mouth in the first place we wouldn't be in this mess. Now let her get herself out of it."

"See you tomorrow," I called. But as I got on the bus, I felt better. Buck and I were right. The project wasn't working out and we had every right to quit. And that's just what I was going to do.

5

If it wasn't for Lizzie's turtle brownies it's possible I might have quit the Creative Social Studies Project that very evening. On the way to Lizzie's I considered volunteering to call Victoria myself and tell her all four of us were through. But Lizzie's turtle brownies are like nothing you've ever eaten before. She manages to melt the caramel just perfectly, so when you bite in you get a thick mouthful of brownie, drenched in melted caramel, and frosted with chocolate-butter frosting. It is so delicious you don't even want to swallow it because then you know it will be gone. When you eat Lizzie's turtle brownies nothing in the world seems bad. That's why, when Lizzie said we'd better get together to discuss the project over turtle brownies, I had agreed. I figured a turtle brownie would certainly give me the courage to face Victoria Chubb.

When I got to Lizzie's house, Buck and Roger had already made a dent in the still-warm pile of brownies. "Are these regular or deep-dish?" Buck was asking Lizzie, as I joined th[ ] family room.

"Regular," Lizzie said. "I never heard of a dish turtle brownies."

"You should invent them," Buck said. "Just like someone invented deep-dish apple pie. You could become famous."

Lizzie shrugged and I got the feeling she wasn't too concerned right now about becoming famous. "These look great," I said, reaching for a brownie.

"When I got done with that reading I had to do something to cheer myself up," Lizzie said, her hand right next to mine as I picked up the brownie.

"Why?" I asked. I couldn't imagine how reading to two blind women could possibly have been as bad as what I'd gone through. "Didn't they listen to you?"

"Oh, they listened all right," Lizzie said. "That's just it. All they did was listen."

"So what's wrong with that?" Buck asked, happily running his tongue along his lips, glazed with caramel. "It's better than what I had to put up with. You should have seen that basketball team."

"And the little girls I tutored were awful," I added. "They just wanted to fool around and complain about their mothers. I was ready to scream when I got done."

"I was ready to cry," Lizzie said.

"I know what you mean," Roger said. "Didn't

Dale say we were supposed to feel good when this was over? Well I felt miserable. Give me maps and a social studies textbook any old day."

"What happened to you?" I asked Roger. "I thought all you had to do was grocery shop. We did that all summer long and you never found it so horrible then."

"This wasn't the same," Roger told us. "First I had to go over to the Cranes' house. Mrs. Crane is in a wheelchair and Mr. Crane looks like he's about eighty years old and they seemed to be embarrassed that I was there. He started telling me how years ago when his grandson came to the house Mrs. Crane would always have homemade cookies ready. But then his grandson moved to California and they don't hear much from him anymore. And he apologized that he didn't have any cookies for me."

"They were probably *glad* you were there, not embarrassed, if they wanted to give you cookies," Buck said.

"No, they were embarrassed," Roger insisted. "Mr. Crane told me the next time I came they'd have the house picked up more. It was sort of messy. And he's got a train set in the basement he wants to show me, but he's got to dust it off first. *I* was embarrassed at that. What does he think I am, some little kid that wants to play with trains? I don't want to go back."

"Me neither," Lizzie agreed. "Agnes and Molly listened to what I was reading, but . . ."

"What did you read them?" Buck interrupted.

"The newspaper," Lizzie said.

"Sports?" Buck asked.

"No," Lizzie said. "I started with the headlines. Then I read the weather. Then I read an article about fall fashions."

"That sounds interesting," I said. "Did they like that one?"

"They liked them all, I guess," Lizzie said. "They listened and they were polite. But they didn't seem to care. Roger's right, they seemed embarrassed by it all. As if they had to do it but it really didn't mean anything to them."

"Next time try the sports section," Buck said. "Sports will mean something."

Lizzie gave Buck an exasperated look and shook her head. "I don't think there's going to be a next time," she said.

For a moment we were all quiet. I knew everyone was thinking the same thing. None of us wanted to continue with the Creative Social Studies Project. But none of us really knew how to get out of it either.

"So what are we going to do?" Roger finally said. "We got into this mess, now we've got to get out of it."

"No we didn't," I argued. "Victoria Chubb got

49

us into this. We're doing all this so she can go to England. And that isn't fair!"

"That's right," Lizzie said. "Victoria got us into this, now let's let Victoria get us out of it."

"How do we do that?" Buck asked, looking longingly at the plate of turtle brownies. There were only three left. Someone would have to go without.

"Go ahead, have one," Lizzie told him. "I'm stuffed."

"Tomorrow we'll tell Victoria not to expect to see us at the creative social studies class anymore," Roger said. "We'll tell her we tried it and we didn't like it. It's up to her to get people to take our place. And if she can't do it, she just won't make it to England."

"Right!" Lizzie and I said together.

"Yea," Buck said weakly.

We all looked at him. "What's wrong with that?" I asked.

"Nothing," Buck said. "Except I kind of like this idea. I guess I agree with Victoria on one thing. I hate maps and reading about other countries just as much as she does. As least this way we're *doing* something, not just listening to some boring teacher."

"But you said the boys you had to teach to play basketball were terrible," I reminded him.

"But still not as terrible as sitting in a social

studies class," Buck said. "There are different kinds of terrible. And don't forget Mr. Ramstead. Remember what Victoria said about him?"

"This is different," Lizzie said. "We're not just quitting because we feel like it. We tried it and it just isn't right for us. It isn't what we thought it would be."

"Before my brother Tommy started working for the Pizza Connection, he worked at a gas station," Roger said. "He thought he'd really like it because he loves cars. But the smell of the gasoline made him feel sick. So he quit. Even my father, who never lets us quit anything, said Tommy's health had to come first."

"How is the Creative Social Studies Project affecting your health?" Buck asked.

"It's making me depressed," Roger said.

"It's making me overeat," Lizzie said. "I had three turtle brownies before you guys even got here."

"And I've chewed off two fingernails since this thing started," I told Buck. "So you see, it *is* affecting our health."

"I bet returning to a social studies class will affect my health," Buck said, looking sadly at the empty plate of turtle brownies.

"You don't have to quit just because we are," Roger said.

"Right," Lizzie agreed. "If you want to work

for Victoria Chubb just so she can take a lovely trip to England with her rich father, go right ahead."

"Yea," I added. "Maybe she'll even let you go with her."

I knew we were being mean to Buck. And he really didn't deserve it. After all, there were some good things about the project and in a way I knew all of us felt badly about quitting. But another thing I knew was that if we'd signed ourselves up for this project we probably wouldn't be giving up so easily. But we hadn't signed ourselves up. Victoria Chubb had taken a chance and lost.

"I would never go to England with Victoria Chubb!" Buck told me, giving me a fierce look. "I don't even like living in the same town with her."

"I was just kidding," I said.

"And I don't want to see her getting away with this any more than you do. So if everyone else is quitting, I will, too," Buck declared.

"Great!" Roger said. "Then it's settled. When we see Victoria tomorrow we'll tell her."

"Right," Lizzie.

"I'll feel a lot better when I'm out of this," I said.

"A social studies class can be a lot worse, I'm telling you," Buck grumbled glumly.

"Don't worry, I'll help you with any homework or projects you get," Roger told him, giving Buck a pat on the back.

"Me, too," Lizzie said. "Whatever you need, Buck."

"Same here," I said. "Just call."

"Yea," said Buck without much enthusiasm. "I will."

And even though I guessed he probably wasn't too happy about our decision, in time I knew he'd realize we'd done the right thing. And that, I figured, would be that.

6

"**H**ave you thought about how you want to celebrate your birthday this year?" my mother asked me the next morning, as she dumped a packet of low-calorie sugar substitute into her steaming mug of coffee. For some strange reason, Lester was still asleep and my dad had already left for work. It was nice to have my mother to myself for a few minutes.

"Not really," I said. "Last year was good, but I'd like to do something different this year."

Last year, when I turned twelve, I invited six girls to stay overnight. My dad took us all to Shakee's where we got to order takeout food — whatever we wanted. Then we brought it back and ate it in my bedroom while we watched videos on TV. At midnight my mother came in with a cake and ice cream, and by the time we finished that and finally fell asleep it was about three o'clock. Everyone who was there said it was the best birthday party they'd ever been to, and even my mother agreed.

"And the best part was that the mess was all in *your* room," she'd told me. "When it was over I didn't have to clean up a thing."

"So you don't want six girls in for an overnight this year, right?" she asked me now.

"I don't think so," I said.

"Do you want to celebrate here or go out somewhere? Maybe just the family? We could go to a nice restaurant and . . ."

"Take Lester to a nice restaurant?" I said. "That wouldn't be any fun. He'd make a mess and a lot of noise and it would ruin everything."

"I suppose you're right," my mother agreed. "It just seems we haven't done much as a family in a while."

"That's because Lester . . ." As if he knew I was talking about him and he wanted to defend himself, my brother let out a good-morning wail from his room upstairs.

"I know," my mother said, getting up to go to him. "I keep forgetting he's only eight months old. Doesn't it seem to you we've had him for longer than that?"

"*Much* longer," I said.

"So think about your birthday," my mother said, as she headed upstairs. "Maybe just you and Dad and I could go out to dinner or to a play. Or you could invite some friends over."

"Could I invite some friends out for dinner?" I asked. A birthday idea was coming to life in my head.

"That's an idea," my mother said.

"To a nice restaurant?" I asked.

"It depends on how nice," my mother called as she hurried off to get Lester.

And suddenly I knew how I wanted to celebrate my birthday. What if I asked Lizzie, Buck, and Roger if they wanted to go out to dinner with me? We could all dress up and my dad could drive us and we could order whatever we wanted using his charge card. I could even call ahead to be sure they had a cake for dessert. The more I thought of it, as I polished off my corn muffin and chocolate milk, the more I liked the idea.

One glance at the kitchen clock told me I'd been daydreaming longer than I realized. I had only two minutes to get to the bus stop. "I think I know what I want for my birthday, Mom," I called upstairs as I raced out.

"Whatever you want, just let me know," she called back. "Have a fun day!"

Which was just what I planned on having. Because already I was picturing myself telling Lizzie all about my birthday plans, and then finding Victoria Chubb and telling her I was quitting the Creative Social Studies Project.

* * *

Some days don't turn out the way you plan them, and this was one of those days. First of all, Lizzie wasn't on the bus. So I ended up sitting with Cindy Lambert, who started complaining right away about Ms. Bugenhagen and the plants we had to grow.

"I don't think it's fair," Cindy said. "I was telling my father about it and he doesn't think it's fair either. In fact, he thinks it's stupid. He thinks I should try to get out of that class."

"I'm getting out of the creative social studies class," I said. "I'm telling them today."

"What's that like?" Cindy asked.

"Oh, you have to do things like tutor or run errands for people," I said.

"That sounds like fun," Cindy said. "Maybe I'll try to get into that. I have Mr. Pender for social studies and he's almost as bad as Ms. Bugenhagen. He has us reading almost a chapter a night and answering all the questions at the end. It took me over an hour last night. What kind of homework does the creative project have?"

"None really," I said. "I mean, I guess the team leaders have to write up reports. But I'm not a team leader."

Cindy's words reminded me of what Buck had said last night, about how a class could be just as bad as the project. I'd forgotten about homework. For a second I thought maybe I should stick with the tutoring. But then I remembered how frustrated I'd felt as Tracey and Ellissa smeared soap all over their faces in the bathroom. And I decided no matter what anyone said, nothing was going to stop me from quitting the project.

A few minutes later, as I started for my homeroom, I spotted Buck peeling an orange and dropping the skin into a trash can in front of the trophy cases in the school lobby. "Hey, Buck," I called. "Have you seen Victoria yet?"

"No," he said. "I was going to look for her at lunch." He held out the orange to me. "Want a piece?" he asked. "I didn't have much time for breakfast today."

"No thanks," I said. "But if you see her before I do, tell her Cindy Lambert might be interested in tutoring. I was talking to her on the bus this morning and she seemed sort of interested."

"You can tell her yourself," Buck said. "Here she comes now." He popped a section of orange into his mouth then called, "Hey, Victoria! Come here. Gina wants to tell you something."

I glared at Buck as Victoria approached us. She gave me a wide smile, her shiny button eyes looking me up and down. Pushing a stray curl off her forehead, she said, "I love your T-shirt, Gina. That color blue is perfect on you."

"It's my mother's," I said. "Since she had a baby it doesn't fit her anymore."

"You're lucky she has good taste," Victoria said. "My mother had to go to this class that tells you how to dress for success. And I still wouldn't wear any of her clothes. Everything is black, navy, or gray. Of course, with my job as team leader, I have to wear more professional-looking things on those days. But really, I love bright colors just like you do."

"That's kind of what I wanted to talk to you about," I said. "About the Creative Social Studies Project. You see — "

"There's nothing to worry about," Victoria interrupted. "I spoke to Mr. Dale and he said you were dressed just fine. For tutoring, in fact, he said it was really good. Little kids like their teachers to look interesting. It holds their attention better."

"That's not — " I began again.

"So I'm sorry I said that to you," Victoria went on quickly. "I guess I was thinking that since I had to look professional, everyone else did, too. But you don't."

I looked helplessly at Buck. He was chewing on an orange slice, but I thought I saw an amused look on his face. Victoria glanced up at the clock, which was just a few minutes away from first period. For a second I got the feeling she knew what I was trying to say and she was purposely not letting me say it. Well she wasn't going to get away with that!

"Look, Victoria," I said. "I don't mind if you didn't like what I wore to tutor. The point is, I don't like tutoring. Those little girls don't want to learn to read. All they want to do is fool around. And I don't like trying to force them to read. So I quit. And so does Buck."

Victoria's dark round eyes widened with disbelief. Two spots of pink flush dotted her cheeks. "But you can't!" she said.

"Yes we can," I said. "Right, Buck?" Buck nodded, but he kept on chewing. "We don't like it. And Lizzie and Roger don't like it either."

"You haven't given it a chance," Victoria said.

"Yes we have," I said. "We all gave it a chance and it turned out horrible. So we're quitting."

"You're supposed to bring any problems to me," Victoria said. "Just tell me what you don't like. That's my job. I have to deal with the problems. It's going to look very bad if my whole team quits without even giving me a chance to help them solve their problems."

I looked at Buck. He shrugged. "My problem is I don't like basketball," he said. "I mean, I like to watch it, and sometimes I like to play. But I really hate coaching it."

"And my problem is I don't want to be a tutor. I don't think I'm any good with little kids. Just this morning I was trying to plan my birthday with my mother, and when she suggested we take my baby brother out to dinner with us I said absolutely not. I don't want some little kid making a mess at my birthday dinner."

"When's your birthday?" Victoria asked.

"In November," I said, wishing I had kept my mouth shut. That was the trouble. When I get excited I start blabbering and I always say too much. "But my birthday isn't the problem. The problem is, I don't want to tutor."

"And Buck doesn't want to coach, right?" Victoria said.

"Right," Buck said.

"Well that's no problem!" Victoria said. A bright smile lit her face. "In fact, I'm glad you came to me. It's simple."

"We quit, right?" I said.

"You don't have to quit," Victoria said. The way she said it made it sound as if she were really giving us great news. "No one has to quit. I just hope the answers to all the problems are this simple," she said happily.

"I don't get it," I said. "What's the answer?"

Victoria grinned. "The answer is, Buck does the tutoring and you do the coaching. It's amazing how sometimes a solution is right in front of your nose. But it takes a team leader to point it out to you."

For a second I couldn't believe my ears. I was to do the coaching! Victoria Chubb had to be crazy. And Buck tutor! She was insane. I looked at Buck, expecting to see him laughing out loud. But to my surprise, he was looking at Victoria with a sort of curious admiration.

61

"Great idea, isn't it?" Victoria said.

"No, it isn't," I said. "I don't want to coach. I don't know a thing about basketball. And I'm sure Buck doesn't want to end up tutoring two little eight-year-olds who just want to have their hair done and talk about nail polish. Do you, Buck?"

"I don't know," said Buck. "It might be sort of interesting."

"Interesting?" I said. "I told you what it was like. It was horrible."

"That's just how it was for you, Gina," Victoria said. "For Buck, it might be totally different. And now that you've tried it out, we know what the problems are. When Buck goes to do it, I'll have some things he can use to make the girls behave better. That's what the team leader's job is."

"You're going to do it?" I asked Buck.

"Anything would be better than having to sit through another class," he said. "Yea, I'll try the tutoring."

"And so you'll do the coaching, right Gina?" Victoria smiled at me. "I think it's really neat. A girl coaching a boys' basketball team. Mr. Dale is going to love this."

"I don't know a thing about basketball!" I cried.

"Leave that to me," Victoria told me. Her mouth puckered into a small smile. "Leave all that to me." The bell rang and she started off. "I'm your team leader. That is part of my responsibility. I'll tell you more later, but right now, I don't want to be late for class. I've got Ms. Delraney and she doesn't appreciate lateness." With that, Victoria was gone, just another head moving down the hallway that was crowded with kids rushing to classes.

I turned to look at Buck. "I can't believe you've done this to me," I said indignantly.

"I didn't do anything," Buck said innocently, pulling a strawberry Pop-tart from his back pocket. He tore open the wrapper and pushed out the tart. "Want a piece?" he asked.

"No, I do not want a piece!" I snapped. "We decided last night, *all four of us*, that we were going to quit," I reminded him. "And you said you didn't want to let Victoria get away with this either. And so what do you do? You take sides with her and let her win again!"

"Not exactly," Buck said. "I said I was going to quit the coaching. Which I did. I didn't say I wasn't going to try something else."

"We said we were going to quit the whole thing," I said. "No one mentioned switching jobs."

"So why didn't you quit the whole thing?" Buck asked.

"Because Victoria didn't give me a chance. Every time I tried to say something, she interrupted and kept right on with what *she* wanted to say. And *you* didn't help matters."

"She doesn't give up, does she?" Buck said. And again, I noticed he said it with a sort of admiration. And that made me madder than anything. Buck and I had been friends for a long time, since kindergarten in fact, and I thought we agreed on how we felt about Victoria Chubb. I couldn't believe he was being such a traitor.

"Well she better come up with something awfully good for this coaching job," I said. "Because if she doesn't, I *am* quitting everything. And I hope you *hate* the tutoring," I said, as I started down the hall. The late bell was ringing, but I didn't care. It seemed a long time since I'd been at home, talking about my birthday plans with my mother. Suddenly, those plans didn't seem too exciting either. I mean, if Buck thought Victoria Chubb was so great, did I really want to celebrate my birthday with him?

For a second I thought I would cry. I was stuck coaching a game I knew nothing about, I was mad at Buck, and Lizzie wasn't in school. It didn't seem things could get much worse.

7

If I learned one thing at school that day, I learned that things can *always* get worse. Right before study hall, which I have third period, I stopped at the phones and called Lizzie. I was sure she'd be as angry as I was when I told her what Victoria had done. *And* when I told her how Buck had gone along with it.

"Hello?" A strange, scratchy voice answered Lizzie's phone.

"Lizzie?" I asked.

"Gina," she squeaked. "I've lost my voice."

"How did that happen?" I asked. "You were fine last night."

"I woke up and it was gone. And I've got a horrible sore throat, too," Lizzie said. "My mom's coming home from work in an hour and taking me in for a strep test."

"Wait until you hear what Victoria Chubb did," I told her. The first bell rang as I quickly related the story of how Victoria had forced me to switch into coaching. And how Buck hadn't even tried to get out of it. "She claims that's her job as team leader," I told Lizzie. "To solve all the problems."

"I wish she could solve my throat problems," Lizzie said. "It hurts so much I can't even eat."

"So do you think you and Roger will quit?" I asked.

"I don't know," Lizzie said. "If I'm going to miss school that's one good thing about the project — at least I won't get behind in any assignments. I'll have enough to catch up on with everything else, without taking on social studies reports, too."

"You mean you're not going to quit?" I cried.

"I don't know," Lizzie said weakly.

I couldn't believe it. What about all the plans we'd made last night? What was wrong with my friends anyway? Why couldn't they stick by what they'd said? I was just about to ask Lizzie that when the second bell rang. And after all, she was sick. It probably wasn't fair to blame her completely.

"Look, I've gotta go. I'll call you tonight," I said. "I hope you feel better."

"Thanks," Lizzie squeaked as I hung up. Yet as I raced toward the study hall, I couldn't help but think that even though I didn't have strep throat I probably felt just as horrible as Lizzie did.

The good thing about study hall is that as long as you don't bother anybody, you don't have to do a thing. Which is exactly what I did. For a while I just sat and stared into my notebook. Finally I picked up my pencil and drew a big circle. That circle was Victoria. Around it I put four smaller circles. Those were the four of us. Together, the four of us circles were bigger than the Victoria circle. Something didn't make sense, and I was trying to figure it out when Mr. Dale poked his head in the door.

"Excuse the interruption," he said, tugging on the tip of his mustache as he looked around the room. His eyes found me. "There she is," he said. "Gina, could I see you for just a few moments?"

"Sure," I said, closing my notebook and gathering up my things.

"Meet me in room 102," Mr. Dale called, handing me a pink hall pass. Then he disappeared up the hall in the opposite direction.

Now what? I wondered as I started toward 102. Could Victoria have told Mr. Dale I wanted to quit, and was he going to sit me down and try to talk me out of it? I wasn't giving in, that was for sure. I would tell him just what had happened and how I felt. And if I had to, I would even mention Victoria's trip to England. I wondered what Mr. Dale would think about that!

"Hey, Gina," a voice called from behind me. I turned around. It was Buck, waving a pink hall pass and grinning like mad. "Isn't this great? I got pulled out of math. Old Sedgwich was just about to ask me to come up to the board and draw some sort of fancy triangle, and Mr. Dale said I had to go to room 102. I knew there was something about this social studies project I liked."

"Good for you," I said. "I got pulled out of study hall. I was right in the middle of something important, too." Even though that wasn't exactly the truth, I was still annoyed at Buck for not standing up to Victoria Chubb with me that morning.

Buck didn't say anything as he pulled open the door of 102 and followed me in. Mr. Dale and Victoria were sitting at the table.

"Have a seat," Mr. Dale told us. "I'm sorry I had to pull you out of your classes."

"No problem," Buck said as we sat down.

"But that's one wonderful thing about this project," Mr. Dale went on. "The rest of the faculty is so enthusiastic about it, they've assured me if emergencies arise, which I hope they won't too often, I can borrow the students involved from class at any time."

"That is wonderful," Buck said happily.

"We'll make this brief," Mr. Dale said. "Victoria has told me there were some difficulties on your first day and that you've requested some changes." He gave Victoria a warm smile. "Actually, I'm glad you had problems. The team leaders need that challenge. And I must admit, your team leader has risen to the occasion brilliantly.

I'll let Victoria herself tell you how she's handled your situation. I know you're going to be as impressed as I am."

Victoria was beaming as she faced Buck. A picture of her, sitting in an elegant English hotel, sipping tea at a table covered with delicious desserts, flashed into my head. I stared down at the scratched wooden table.

"From what Gina told me about those little girls," Victoria said, "I figured we needed something good to get their attention. If they like fashion and nail polish, we should let them study that. So I asked Mr. Dale if we could let them learn to read that stuff instead of books. And he said it was a good idea. Then I remembered how good you are at art." She grinned at Buck. "Remember those great signs you did to advertise Aces last summer?"

Buck was giving Victoria a blank look, but she ignored it and continued. "So I called home and asked our housekeeper to bring me a few things I thought would help you "

Housekeeper? I thought. Victoria has a housekeeper?

From the floor by her chair Victoria brought up a big paper bag. "These are old *Teen Years* magazines I'm going to give you to use," she explained. "And here are some things that could help you teach the girls to read colors." From the bag she began pulling out a bunch of half-filled bottles of old nail polish, which she lined up along the table. "My mother is a nail polish freak," Victoria explained. "She'll never miss these."

Buck watched her dumbfounded. Mr. Dale was nodding like crazy and smiling in approval. Buck reached over and picked up a bottle of nail polish. "Scarlet Scream?" he said.

"Isn't that great!" Victoria exclaimed. "Look at this one. Royal Ruby Red. And here's one called Popsicle Pink. Those girls are going to love this."

Maybe Tracey and Ellissa would love it, but by the look in Buck's eyes I could see he didn't love it. "You really want me to do this?" he asked Mr. Dale.

"Creative teaching is what it's all about, Edward," Mr. Dale said, calling Buck by the name only his parents and teachers used. "Believe me, I know. It's different, but wait until you see the results."

Buck's face had turned about the same shade as the Popsickle Pink nail polish, and I have to confess, I felt a little sorry for him. But it was his own fault. If he'd spoken up to Victoria this morning by the trophy case, he wouldn't be sitting here now reading bottles of nail polish.

"Now for you, Gina," Victoria said. "You said you didn't know anything about basketball, so I went to the library and got out two books that will tell you everything you need to know."

70

She handed me the books, both of which had pictures on the cover of guys running around on a basketball court. I flipped through one. "Offensive strategy?" I said, making an unpleasant face.

"Don't let the words scare you," Mr. Dale said. "Basketball is a fun game — you must have played it. Just wait till you pull that team together. And a girl coach on a boys' team is becoming very popular. In fact, last year's High School Coach of the Year was a woman!"

Mr. Dale's voice was getting that excited tone that made him so hard to disagree with. Buck was leafing through a *Teen Years* magazine and I could tell he wasn't going to say anything, so I closed the book and said, "Is that all?"

"One more thing," Victoria said cheerily. "Buck also said he'd had some trouble keeping the names of the boys straight. So I asked around in the gym and Mr. Peters said he had just the things we needed."

From her bag she pulled out what looked like big cotton bibs. I had worn them before in gym class. They were the kind you slip on over your head and tie at the waist. Gym teachers use them to set up teams.

"Bibs?" I said.

"They're called *pinnies*," Victoria told me. "And Mr. Peters said we could write on these, so I put each of the boys' names on in marker."

Sure enough, there were two Timmys, two Eddies and two Peters. "Thanks," I said, without much enthusiasm.

Mr. Dale stood up and ran his fingers through his long, thin hair. "This is the sort of teamwork I had hoped I'd see. But I never dreamed I'd be seeing it so soon," he told us. "Now I have a phone call to make. So you can all head back to where you belong."

The second he left us, packing up nail polish and basketball pinnies, I turned to Victoria. She was smiling smugly, looking so pleased with herself that I wanted to smack her. "Don't think these books are going to make that big a difference," I said. "I still want to quit. Just because I'm going to do the coaching tomorrow, doesn't mean that I'm going to do it for the whole ten weeks."

"Then we'll let Roger try it, and you can run the errands," she said smoothly.

"I don't want to run errands," I said. "And Roger doesn't want to coach basketball. He hates basketball more than anyone."

"Here, Buck," Victoria said, handing him the bag with the magazines and nail polish. "You better take this."

"I'm not walking around school with a bag full of nail polish," Buck grumbled. "You take it."

For a second I thought Victoria was going to get mad. I wished she would, because I knew there was no way she could make Buck carry that bag and, just for once, I wanted to see her have to give in to us. But she didn't.

"No problem," she said. "Since you'll be tutoring right here in 102 I'll just leave it here. No one uses this room except creative social studies this year anyway."

"See ya," Buck said as he headed for the door. I followed him into the hall.

"So now what do you think about the tutoring?" I asked. "Do you really want to teach nail polish reading?"

"Not especially," Buck said. "But what can we do? And I'll tell you one thing, I'm not going back to math class." He held up his pink pass and gave it a mock kiss. "I'm going straight to the cafeteria. I may have to teach nail polish reading, but I'm also going to be the first one in line for lunch. You coming?"

"Not yet," I said. "I've got to stop at my locker first."

Buck took off and I started down the hall to my locker. Just like he didn't want to walk around school with a bag full of nail polish and *Teen Years* magazines I wasn't too thrilled about carrying those basketball bibs around either. But leave it to Victoria Chubb to see that I had to, I thought, as I shoved them into my locker along with the two books, and gave the door an extra hard slam. Leave it to Victoria Chubb.

* * *

"Any more thoughts on how you want to celebrate your birthday?" my mother asked, passing the scalloped potatoes to my dad at dinner that night.

"I had a great idea," I said. "I was thinking maybe Lizzie, Buck, Roger, and I could go out for dinner at a nice restaurant."

My mother smiled and my dad said, "I don't see any problem with that."

"But Lizzie's sick and Buck's been doing some dumb things lately," I continued glumly. "So maybe I'll just forget it."

My parents looked at me with concern. "What's wrong with Lizzie?" my mother asked.

"What kind of dumb things has Buck been up to?" my dad wanted to know.

"Lizzie might have strep throat," I said. "I'm going to call her after dinner and find out. And Buck won't speak up to Victoria Chubb so we're still in the Creative Social Studies Project. Except instead of *me* doing the tutoring, Buck is. But I'm coaching the basketball team! *Me!* I don't know anything about basketball. We've played a few times in gym, but I don't know enough to show anybody else."

I knew my voice was beginning to get loud for the dinner table because Lester had stopped playing with his plastic spoon and was giving me a curious look. But I didn't care.

"So what does Victoria give me?" I went on.

74

"These dumb books about basketball that I don't understand. How do I know what double dribbling is? Or a lay up? Or chest passes and bounce passes? And I don't care!"

"It's totally logical," my father said. "A chest pass is just that. You hold the ball in front of your chest and pass it to someone. And with a bounce pass you let it bounce once on the way to the person you're passing it to."

"It may be logical to you but it's not logical to me," I said.

"Once you start playing it will all make sense," my father said.

"But I'm not going to be playing," I explained. "I'm supposed to be coaching. How can I coach if I don't know how to *play*?"

For a second my father just looked thoughtfully over the piece of bread he was buttering. Then he said, "Well, I guess you'll just have to play. How about it? Want me to show you a thing or two about basketball?"

So right after dinner my father changed into his sweats and an old pair of running shoes. I put on a pair of baggy jeans, my old yellow sweatshirt with the smile face and *Have a nice day!* written on it, and sneakers. Somewhere in the garage my father found an old basketball. "This was a top-quality ball in its day," he told me proudly, giving it a bounce on the driveway. "See that, it doesn't even need air."

"Where are we going?" I asked, as we got into the car.

"I'm pretty sure there's a basket behind the old Saint Michael's School," my dad said as we drove up my street. "It won't be in great shape because the school's closed. But it should be empty."

Sure enough, at the end of the parking lot next to the deserted school there was a basket. "This lot's a little rough," my father said, giving the ball a trial bounce. "But for what we need to do it's just fine."

"Yea," I said. I still wasn't sure just what we needed to do. But at least there was no one around to see us do it.

"Now watch me," my father instructed. My dad is about average height for a man. When I was little, it seemed to me he was a giant. But as I've grown taller, he hasn't seemed so big. Now, however, as I watched him bouncing the basketball and heading toward the basket, he suddenly seemed pretty big again.

"Look at this," he called. He ran by the basket and without even slowing down dropped the ball through it with one hand. "That's called a jump shot," he said. "Let me show you a lay up."

This time he got real close to the basket. He held the ball with his right hand, jumped up and, looking as if he were almost climbing into the basket, dropped the ball through it.

"Gee, Dad. That's great." My father was beaming.

"Never guessed your old dad was a pretty good athlete in his day, did you?" he said, jumping up again to drop the ball through the basket. "Not that I ever played any real serious basketball. But I always enjoyed meeting the guys in the park after supper and shooting a few."

"I knew you were a good runner," I said. My father runs in the neighborhood a couple of nights a week and on Sunday mornings he meets some of his friends and they run together. Afterward they always stop for bagels with cream cheese, which my mother says probably cancels out the benefits of the run.

"Here," he called. My dad threw the ball to me. When I tried to catch it, it bounced away from me. "Don't be afraid of the ball," he said. "That's the first rule of basketball. Confidence. So," he continued, "the object of the game is to get as many baskets as you can. That's called *offense*. At the same time you try to keep the other team from getting the ball. That's *defense*. The most important thing to remember about basketball is that it's a *team* sport. As my old high school gym teacher used to say, 'In the word *team* there's no *I*.' Get it?"

"I get it," I said. "One person shouldn't hog the ball."

I started to bounce the ball, hitting it with the palm of my hand. "Am I dribbling OK?" I asked.

"Loosen up," my father said. "You're too stiff. And just use the tips of your fingers, not your whole palm. Here, dribble it up to me, then try to make a basket."

Trying to use just the tips of my fingers, I dribbled the ball to my dad. I shot it at the basket, but it hit the rim and came bouncing back to me. "Try it again," my dad said. "Concentrate. Make eye contact with the basket and don't take your eyes off it until you've completed the shot."

I tried it three more times. Three times I missed.

"Don't give up," my dad said. "Keep trying."

This time I stared right at the basket. I threw the ball at it and sure enough, it went in. "Hey!" I cried. "I did it!" Actually, it was kind of fun. Watching that ball sail through the basket gave me a neat feeling and made me want to try it again. I missed twice, but on the third try it went swooshing through. I was surprised that I actually felt a little thrill watching the ball skim through the net.

"Of course, in a real game, you'll have the other team jumping around in front of you trying to keep you away from the basket," he said. "But for now, let's practice some of the basic moves."

For over an hour my dad and I practiced. The

more I got used to touching the ball, the more I felt I could control it. And my dad was a good coach. When I did something wrong, he told me. But when I did something right he got almost as excited as I did. "Beautiful lay up!" he'd shout, or "Gina, that was a great pass!"

It was getting dark when my dad and I finally left Saint Michael's playground. "That was a good workout," my dad said. His cheeks were ruddy and a trickle of sweat ran down the side of his face.

"How do you think I did?" I asked.

"For a beginner, you did just fine," my dad said. "Tomorrow, when you start coaching, teach the guys the same things we worked on tonight. Your dribbling is pretty good, and you're passing pretty well."

"How about the jump shot?" I asked.

"You can show them that. They'll want to start making baskets right away so give them each a chance to dribble up to the basket and then take a turn shooting. That's what teams do for a warm-up before a real game."

I pushed up the sleeves of my sweatshirt as we got into the car. I was sweating, too, but it felt good. And at least I felt as if I knew a little bit about basketball. When I got home I'd read some more from the books Victoria had given me. But basketball, I knew, wasn't the sort of thing you could learn by reading. You had to play it.

"Thanks, Dad," I said, as we drove out of the parking lot. "This really helped."

"I liked it, too," my father said. "I needed the exercise and I'd forgotten how much I like the game. You know, Gina, if you're going to be coaching these guys for ten weeks, you're going to have to keep in shape and keep your game up. Maybe we should do this more often."

I looked at my father and smiled. "I was hoping you might suggest that," I said. "Maybe we could come over here again tomorrow night."

"Tomorrow night's fine with me." My father grinned. "Who ever would have thought my fashion-plate daughter would turn out to be a basketball coach?" he said with a laugh as we headed for home.

8

The next morning Lizzie was on the bus. "It wasn't strep," she told me, still sounding a little hoarse, but much happier, as I slid into the seat next to her. "But I really shouldn't talk too much. The doctor said I could come back to school as long as I don't overdo it. So I'd better save my voice for reading to the blind women."

"That's okay, I'll talk," I said, glad for the chance. "First of all, I can't believe I'm coaching. I've got shorts on under this skirt," I told Lizzie, pulling up the hem of my short denim skirt so she could see the baggy shorts I'd put on. "And look." From around my neck I pulled a gold chain with a silver whistle on it. "I found this at home." I gave it one short, strong blow. It made a loud, sharp screech and several heads turned toward us to see what the noise was. Lizzie and I giggled as I tucked it away.

"And I can't believe Buck is going to be teaching with nail polish either," I said.

"What?!" Lizzie cried.

I told her about Victoria's tutoring plan and she couldn't believe it.

"And Buck's going along with it?" she asked.

"Yesterday he was. Maybe he's changed his mind, though."

But Buck hadn't changed his mind. He was waiting by the trophy cases when Lizzie and I walked into school. Victoria was with him.

"Gina!" she called. "Come here for a second. I've got some great news for you."

"I bet," I mumbled to Lizzie as we walked toward them. It was ridiculous, but my stomach was starting to give little hops and I had the feeling I was entering a classroom to take an important test, instead of just walking through the school lobby to talk to another student. Why did I let Victoria affect me that way?

"Did you read the books?" she asked me.

"Yea," I said. "But you don't learn to play basketball by reading books."

"I know that," Victoria said. "So I've got a few more things that will help you. *Incentives* I think you'd call them in business."

"Incentives?" I questioned.

"You know how teachers give stickers and stars when kids do good on tests? Those are incentives. I've come up with a few incentives for you to give your team."

"What are they?" I asked. Something told me

I wasn't going to like Victoria's idea of incentives any more than I liked most of her ideas.

"First of all, I've given your team a name. The Echoes. How do you like it?"

"The Echoes?" I asked. "It doesn't make sense."

"It makes perfect sense," Victoria replied. "There are two Timmys, two Eddies, and two Peters. Get it? The Echoes?"

"I get it," I said. Actually it was sort of clever. But I certainly wouldn't give Victoria the satisfaction of saying that.

"And I'm going to design a team T-shirt they can wear for the tournament," Victoria went on. "And if they win the tournament they'll get a pizza party. So what do you think?"

"Tournament!" I cried. "What tournament?"

Buck was trying not to look too relieved that he'd given up the coaching and even Lizzie looked astounded.

"It's not going to be any big deal," Victoria said. "Some of the other kids in the project are working with teams, too. Henry Richter has a group down in the girls' gym, and Tammi Chen has a group outside, and so we group leaders thought it would be fun if . . ."

"Fun!" I exclaimed. "Fun for whom? It's not fun for me!"

"Now Gina," Victoria said calmly. "You haven't even met the team yet. Think how excited they'll be to know they could get a pizza party if they play well. It will make your job easier to have something to bribe them with — "

"Hold on a second, Victoria," I said, my voice tense. "While I *might* go along with the tournament, I'm definitely not going to try to *bribe* the team."

"OK, OK, calm down," Victoria said quickly. "Forget about the pizza party if you want to. But you have to admit the rest of my ideas are great. The tournament will give them something to shoot for. By giving them a name and T-shirts you bring them together. My mother manages a big sales team and she told me that's how they make their goals. And they sell millions of dollars worth of stuff."

"It might work," Lizzie said hopefully.

"I bet it could," Buck agreed.

I knew my friends were just trying to make me feel better about the tournament, but they were actually making me feel worse. It seemed as if they were agreeing with Victoria — instead of sticking up for me. But I suppose there was no reason to do that because no matter what happened now, I had to coach that team today. Mr. Dale knew about it, Mr. Ramstead knew about it, and Victoria Chubb knew.

"We'll see," I grumbled as the bell for homeroom rang. I was glad to escape. Even though Lizzie and Buck were my close friends, I felt very alone. They didn't seem to see what Victoria was doing. And everything she was doing was for herself, so she could look good and go on a trip to England. And there didn't seem to be any way to stop her from getting away with it.

I was in no hurry to get to the gym last period that afternoon and so I walked slowly on purpose. That was a mistake. By the time I got there Timmy, Eddie, and Peter, and Timmy, Eddie, and Peter were racing around screaming and fighting over the one basketball someone had left in the gym. They hardly looked at me as I walked in. They were still waiting for Buck.

For a second I just stared at them. I started to get that same helpless feeling I'd gotten with Ellissa and Tracey. I didn't know how to make these kids do what I wanted them to. In fact, I wasn't even sure I *knew* what I wanted them to do. What would Victoria Chubb do if she were in my place, I wondered? Take over, I thought glumly, like she always does.

Suddenly my anger at her returned. I looked down at the silver whistle hanging around my neck. I gave it a mighty blast. Startled, the six boys froze as their heads turned toward me.

"What'd you do that for?" One of the boys, a skinny blond with untied sneakers, was scowling at me.

I scowled back. "I did it because I'm your coach," I said.

The blond boy made a face. "You're not our coach. Buck's our coach. You're a girl."

"Buck and I have switched jobs," I said. "He's tutoring. I'm coaching."

"We want Buck." A small black boy flashed his angry brown eyes at me, while the red-haired kid next to him grumbled "Yea, yea," as he shot me dirty looks.

"We want Buck," the first boy began to chant.

"We want Buck!" Two of the others joined in.

I wanted to turn around and run out of the gym. Instead I gave another short screech on my whistle. Startled, they quieted down. "Look," I said, trying to sound as tough as I could. "Do you want to stand here arguing all afternoon? Or do you want to shoot some hoop?" I knew that was what the guys on the bus always said if they were going to play basketball after school.

For a second no one answered. Then the black boy said, "I want to shoot some hoop."

"Then you have to do what I tell you," I said gruffly. Quickly I pulled the pinnies out of the bag. "Every player has to wear one of these. That way I'll know your names. Which one is Timmy S.?"

The blond boy reached up and took the pinny. "You mean we have to wear bibs?" he asked, making a face.

"They're called pinnies. And tie those sneakers, too," I snapped. Without any argument Timmy S. put on his bib and bent down to tie his sneakers.

86

"Timmy P." The black boy took the pinny. Eddie L. was the redhead, his face marker-smudged; Eddie K. had spiked hair; Peter G. was the shortest; and Peter L. wore glasses.

"Now," I said, when they'd all put on their pinnies and stood looking at me. "In order to learn to play basketball we have to learn some basic things. The first thing we have to learn is how to dribble. Watch me."

Trying to remember everything my father had shown me the night before, I took the ball and gave it a bounce. I tried to use just the tips of my fingers as I bounced the ball up the gym floor toward the basket. I was a little clumsy, but the boys watched me in silence. When I got to the basket I stopped. "Now watch how I keep my eye on the basket," I called to them. "You have to concentrate." I tossed the ball up, it hit the rim and came tumbling back at me. I grabbed for it and missed.

"You won't always be able to make a basket," I said, as I fumbled for the ball. Looking up at the basket I tried again. The ball bounced off the rim. "Even the professional players miss sometimes. But you have to keep trying."

This time I took careful aim. I pushed the ball with the tips of my fingers as I'd seen my father doing the night before. The ball slipped through the basket and the boys clapped.

"It's your turn," I told them. "I want each one

of you to dribble the ball up to the basket and take a shot. We'll try that for awhile, then I'll show you the chest pass."

"Wow," said Timmy P. "You sure know a lot about basketball."

"More than Buck even," Eddie L. added, as he took the ball and started to bounce it.

"Don't use the palm of your hand, just the fingertips," I called to him. I smiled to myself. Even if it was sort of an act, it looked like I was pulling it off! It did seem I knew a lot about basketball — a lot more than Buck even.

"See you in two days," I called to the boys forty minutes later as they started down the hall from the gym to go back to their school.

" 'Bye, Coach," Eddie L. called.

I couldn't believe how well the practice had gone. Once the boys saw I meant business they got very serious about their playing. And when I told them about the tournament they were very excited. "We're going to win," Peter G. announced, handing me his pinny as he left. "I'm going right home now and practice."

"Me, too," Timmy P. called.

I headed to my locker. I couldn't wait to tell Lizzie all that had happened, but I didn't see her in the crowd of kids rushing to their lockers before going home. I did see Buck.

"Hey, Buck," I called. "How'd the tutoring go?"

From the look on Buck's face I didn't have to guess the answer. He looked as pleased as I felt. "Great," he said. "The nail polish was a big hit. We made color charts and the girls read every one back to me. Next week we're going to do some sketches of hairdos. And then they want to put together a fashion magazine. It's really fun."

"The coaching was fun, too," I said. "We did dribbling and chest passes today. Next time I want to start bounce passes and . . ."

"So how'd it go?" I spun around to find Victoria Chubb standing behind Buck and me.

"Not bad," I said, trying to sound as cool as possible.

"Real good!" Buck said, not covering his excitement very well.

"I'm not surprised," Victoria said smugly. Her eyes sparkled and her mouth was pinched in a self-satisfied grin. "Those ideas I came up with were really great, weren't they? Didn't I tell you I could do it? I knew I could use Buck's artistic talent somehow on this project. And having a girl coach a boys' basketball team is a brilliant idea, if I do say so myself. Mr. Dale will have to give me an A now."

Of course I should have known Victoria would take all the credit. "Ideas are no good unless you have people who can carry them out," I said. I could feel a warm flush beginning on my cheeks and at the base of my neck.

"But my ideas were great, weren't they?" Victoria insisted.

"Yea, they really were," Buck said. "Tracey and Ellissa loved the nail polish idea. And the *Teen Years* magazines were a big hit with them, too."

"How about the basketball books, Gina?" Victoria asked.

"Actually they didn't help me at all," I said. "Basketball is not something you can learn by reading. You have to play. Luckily my father was a basketball star in college," I continued, exaggerating a bit. "He's showing me everything I need to know about the game."

Buck looked impressed, but Victoria just said, "I bet they loved being called the Echoes. And Gina, did you tell them about the tournament?"

"I mentioned it," I said.

"That will make a big difference, too, you'll see," Victoria went on confidently. "Well, I better look for Lizzie and Roger. Since I've solved all your problems, I can work on theirs now."

I watched Victoria's curly head as it disappeared in the direction of Lizzie's locker. Then I turned to Buck. "How can she be so obnoxious?" I moaned.

"I don't know." Buck shrugged, and I realized that for some reason, lately Buck didn't see Victoria the same way I did. "I didn't know your father was a basketball star," he said.

"He was," I mumbled.

"What college team did he play for?"

"I don't remember," I said.

"How can you not remember something like that?" Buck demanded.

"Well excuse me for forgetting something," I snapped.

"You're not excused," Buck snapped back. "What's wrong with you anyhow? I just asked an innocent question."

"There's nothing wrong with me," I cried. "It's what's wrong with *you*!"

"What's wrong with me?" Buck asked.

Stupidly I spoke without thinking. "What's wrong with you," I told Buck, "is that I think you have a big crush on Victoria Chubb!"

For a second Buck just stared at me. His round, happy face turned shocked and angry. "And what's wrong with *you*," Buck snapped back at me, "is that you're crazy." With that, he abruptly turned away and started off in the direction of the lockers.

For a moment I stood alone. I swallowed as I felt my eyes begin to water. Why had I said that to Buck? Why was I wrecking my friendship with him after all this time? Now he'd never want to go out to eat with me on my birthday.

After dinner that night I called Lizzie and invited her to come over. Then I told my father I had too much homework to do so I couldn't practice basketball, and I shut myself in my room with a jumbo bag of corn chips and a two-liter bottle of grape soda. By the time Lizzie arrived the chips were half gone and the soda was starting to make me feel queasy.

"Didn't you eat dinner tonight?" Lizzie asked me.

"Yes, I ate dinner tonight," I said irritably. Then I stopped myself. I'd already gotten Buck mad at me. I didn't want to lose Lizzie, too. "Sorry, Lizzie," I said. "I'm just in a horrible mood today." I told her about coaching basketball that day and how Victoria had taken all the credit; how Buck had almost agreed with Victoria; and how I'd told Buck I thought he had a crush on Victoria.

"What did Buck say?" Lizzie asked.

"He said I was crazy. But the other thing is, for my birthday my mother said I could do whatever I wanted. So I was going to invite you, Buck, and Roger to go out to a fancy restaurant for dinner. Now Buck probably won't want to go."

"Buck, pass up food?" Lizzie laughed. "Of course he'll go. He'll have forgotten all about it by then."

Suddenly I felt better. Lizzie was that type of friend. She could always say something to make me realize things weren't as bad as I thought. I reached for a handful of chips as Lizzie poured herself a glass of soda. "You really think so?" I asked.

"For a meal at a restaurant, I guarantee it," Lizzie said.

"So how did the reading go today?" I asked her. "Any better?"

"It was different," Lizzie said. "I got there and I really wasn't in the mood to read. I'd just come from Ms. Delraney's room and she had given us this poetry assignment to do. Plus my voice was still hoarse. So I started to read and all of a sudden Agnes stopped me."

"She didn't like how you were reading?" I asked.

"No, she just thought something was wrong with me. She could tell by my voice. So I ended up telling them the whole thing."

"You told them you didn't want to do the reading?"

"Not exactly. I told them about my problems with Ms. Delraney, how I don't know anything about poetry, and how I need good grades if I'm going to get into a good law school."

"Do you think that was right?" I asked. "I mean, should you be telling them all your problems when they have problems of their own?"

"I know what you mean," Lizzie said. "But it turned out that Agnes loves poetry. She's even written some of her own. So next time she's going to bring in a couple of books that she thinks I'd like. And she said she'd help me with my paper. We're going to start working on it next time."

"That sounds wonderful," I said. "Have you told Victoria?"

"Yes. That's the real problem. She wasn't sure it was such a good idea. She said we were supposed to be helping these people, not having them help us. She was going to ask Mr. Dale what he thinks."

"Since it wasn't her idea, naturally she doesn't think it's any good," I said.

"But the funny thing," Lizzie went on, "was how excited Agnes and Molly got when they saw they were getting to do something for me. It's the most excitement I've seen from them since we started. I got the feeling they didn't like me doing everything for them. They seemed really anxious to get going on this paper."

"Then you should let them do it. If it makes them feel useful, then it has to be good."

"I hope so," Lizzie said. "It would help me, too. But if Victoria . . ."

"Forget Victoria," I said, raising my glass of soda for a toast. "Victoria needs to know who's in charge here. It's not her," I said bravely. After all, Victoria was miles away. "It's the four of us."

Lizzie looked at me quizzically. "Right," she said a little uncertainly. She lifted her glass so it touched mine. "It's the four of us."

9

For the next few weeks everyone seemed a lot happier with the Creative Social Studies Project than they had been at first. At least Lizzie, Buck, and I were. Lizzie handed in her first paper to Ms. Delraney and got an A minus. For Ms. Delraney this is some sort of record. It was a joke around school that she had never learned to write the letter A, so when Lizzie got the paper back about a dozen kids wanted to get a look at it. They said it was probably the first A Ms. Delraney had ever written.

"I never could have done it without Agnes," Lizzie told me, riding home one day. "Not that she tells me what to write, but when we read a poem she has a way of making me see things I never would have seen if I'd read it by myself."

"Do you think it's because she's blind?" I asked.

"What do you mean?" Lizzie asked.

"I mean, do you think she sees things differently in a poem because she can't see them with her eyes?"

"Not really," Lizzie said. "I think she just has to use her imagination a lot, so she's used to doing it more than I am. And I think she's a really smart lady. She's read just about every book the library had in braille and listened to all their books on tape."

"I didn't even know the library had books like that," I said.

"I guess they don't have too many," Lizzie told me. "Agnes and Molly are always complaining about that. That's why they joined this reading project at school. They thought maybe we could read the best-sellers. But it hasn't exactly worked out that way. Although they told me they like helping me with my papers. So I'm going to let them. It seems to make everybody happy."

"My basketball team has been the same way," I said. "I don't think the boys expected to have a girl for a coach. But they act like they don't mind it. And they love basketball. They've gotten to be pretty good, too."

"And Buck's happy. He told me yesterday," Lizzie said. "He's putting together a fashion magazine with those girls. He thinks he might want to be a clothes designer someday."

"Buck!" I cried. "Buck — who doesn't own a T-shirt without a hole in it — wants to be a fashion designer!"

"Yep," Lizzie said as we approached her corner. "That same Buck."

The bus lurched to a stop and Lizzie got up. "I'll call you tonight after dinner," she said as she got off.

But it turned out she talked to me that night before dinner. And it turned out I called her.

"Victoria Chubb just called you," my mother said, as I yanked open the refrigerator door to get myself a snack.

"Victoria Chubb called me?" I asked. "What did she want?"

"I don't know," my mother said. She was letting Lester crawl around on the kitchen floor while she chopped up lettuce and tomatoes and grated cheese to make tacos for dinner. "She said to have you call her back as soon as you got in. She sounded a little urgent."

I didn't like the sound of that. I wasn't crazy about the fact that Victoria had called me in the first place. But to know she sounded urgent made me very uneasy. "I suppose I'll have to call her back," I said.

"And then set the table," my mother called as I headed upstairs to use the phone.

"Chubb residence." A woman's brisk voice answered at Victoria's. I guessed it was the housekeeper.

"Can I please speak to Victoria?"

"May I ask who is calling?"

"Gina," I said.

"And your last name, please?"

"Lazzaro," I said. I was waiting for her to ask my height and weight, too, but she didn't.

"Just a moment, please. I'll see if I can find her."

The line went quiet and I waited. Although it wasn't more than a minute or so, it seemed I waited for an awfully long time. How big is Victoria's house if it takes that long to find her, I wondered.

Finally, Victoria came to the phone. "Hello, Gina?"

"My mother said you called me," I said.

"We have a problem," Victoria told me. "I'm calling a special meeting tomorrow to discuss it. But I thought I'd let everybody know so they could think about it overnight. Sometimes the best ideas come to people in dreams. If you think about the problem right before you go to sleep the answer may come to you while you're sleeping. Do you dream in color or in black-and-white, Gina?"

"I don't know," I said. "I don't think I dream at all. If I do have dreams I forget them when I wake up."

I was not about to tell Victoria Chubb that when I was a little kid I kept having this nightmare about blue and purple monkeys chasing me, and I'd woken up screaming so much that my mother took me to a doctor. The doctor said she thought maybe the dream came from watching *The Wizard of Oz* too often, and thinking that the monkeys were after me. Luckily right after I went to that doctor I outgrew the nightmare, and I haven't paid much attention to my dreams since then.

"So what's the problem?" I asked Victoria.

"Roger," she told me.

"Roger?" I asked. "What's wrong with Roger?"

"Roger wants to quit the Creative Social Studies Project," Victoria said. "He told me today. And do you know how that will look for our team? And what am I going to write in my report? I've solved every other problem on this team. Now I've got to solve this one."

I didn't say anything. My first thought was that Roger's problem was Victoria's problem, not my problem. But Roger was my friend. If I could help him in some way I was willing to do it. Still, I wasn't giving up my basketball team!

"So what do you want me to do?" I asked.

"Since you are a member of this team," Victoria said a little huffily, "I thought you could think of ways to help Roger."

"He can't have my coaching job," I said. "He hates basketball anyway. But if that's what you are thinking, I won't switch."

"I know," Victoria said. "I already suggested that to him. And he doesn't want any part of the tutoring or the reading either. He's making this very hard for me."

"What doesn't he like about running errands?" I asked.

"He doesn't think Mr. and Mrs. Crane like the idea that they need someone to help them out. He thinks they're embarrassed when he comes over, so he feels bad. But really, Gina. I don't see what he's complaining about. He can't expect to be happy all the time."

As usual, Victoria was making me mad. Of course no one was happy all the time. But why should Roger have to be unhappy just because she'd signed him up for something he didn't want to do in the first place?

"Roger is a very sensitive person," I told her sharply. "And since you're the team leader I think you should find some way to see that he's happy in his job. And if you can't do that then I think he has every right to quit. And I'll tell him that, too."

"Come on, Gina!" Victoria wailed so loudly into the phone that I had to hold it away from my ear.

"What can I do?" I asked.

"Just try to think of something. And I'm going to call Buck and Lizzie and have them try to think of something, too. And tomorrow we'll have an emergency meeting. We can talk about our ideas then."

"I don't know if I'll have any ideas to talk about," I said. "If Roger wants to quit maybe we should let him quit."

"Mr. Dale isn't going to like that," Victoria

warned. "And Mr. Ramstead isn't either. And the Cranes are depending on Roger."

"Gina! Come down and set the table. Now!" For once I was glad to hear my mother calling me to get off the phone.

"I've got to go," I told Victoria.

"Think about this before you go to sleep and tomorrow let me know what you dream," Victoria said. "I know there's a way to make Roger stay. The meeting is first thing tomorrow morning in front of the trophies."

I hurried down to set the table, then I called Lizzie. She'd already talked to Victoria. "Teamwork," Lizzie said. "That's what she told me she wanted from us. Teamwork to solve this problem with Roger. Which is really *her* responsibility."

"I'm going to tell him to quit," I said. "It will serve Victoria right. Did she tell you to think about it before you went to sleep and see if the answer came to you in your dreams?"

"Yes," said Lizzie with a giggle. "Where does she get her ideas?"

"I don't know," I said. Then my mother called me for dinner so I said good-bye to Lizzie. And for the rest of the evening I didn't think about it anymore.

After dinner my dad and I went over to the basketball court to practice. "Tonight we're going to do a dribble drill," my father announced as we got out of the car. From the trunk he pulled out four lawn chairs. He set them up on the court and said to me, "Now think of them as players on the opposite team. You've got to dribble around them to get to your basket."

The first time I did pretty well, although I was concentrating so much on getting around the chairs that I wasn't in a good position to shoot when I finally got to the basket. I missed by a mile.

"Not bad," my dad said. "Now try it again." This time he moved the chairs closer to each other. Suddenly the court felt very crowded. And then I realized, this was how it would feel in a real game. Every player would be pushing to get closer to the ball. Now when I tried to dribble to the basket I knocked over two of the chairs.

"Try it again," my father said. "Take it slow until you get the feel of it. Then speed up."

By the end of our hour of practice I had it down pretty well. And I was excited about trying this drill tomorrow with the Echoes.

That night I did have a dream I remembered, a good dream. The Echoes were playing in a big tournament and every time they got the ball they dribbled up the court and made a basket. A huge crowd was watching, cheering every play. In the end, the Echoes won by a hundred points and the crowd went wild. Of course, in my dream it was pretty easy for the Echoes — the other team was made up of chairs.

The following morning Victoria was right where she said she'd be, by the trophy case, when Lizzie and I entered school. Buck was there with her and they were both eating peanut candies from a huge bag Buck was holding. He offered some to Lizzie and me.

"No thanks," I said. "I just finished breakfast."

"And I don't want sugar sitting on my teeth all morning long," Lizzie said.

"Then you should do what I do," Victoria told her. From her large leather purse she pulled out a purple toothbrush and small tube of toothpaste. "My mother told me no successful woman travels without a toothbrush and toothpaste. Do you know how easy it is to get bad breath? Or have food stuck in your teeth? And that is so gross!"

Actually, carrying a toothbrush and toothpaste wasn't such a bad idea. But rather than let her know I agreed with her I said, "So what's going on with Roger? Have you come up with an answer to that, Victoria?"

"I have a few things I'm considering," she said. "But I wanted to hear what everyone else thought before I did anything. So, what do you guys think?" she asked Lizzie and me.

I shrugged. "I don't know," I said.

"Did you have any good dreams last night?" Victoria asked me.

"Victoria, what I dreamed last night has nothing to do with Roger." I was feeling annoyed. Didn't she ever give up?

"You never know," Victoria said. "What was your dream?"

"I dreamed that the Echoes won the tournament one hundred to nothing. But the other team's players were chairs, so it was pretty easy for them to win."

Victoria frowned. "Chairs?" she said. "I wonder what that means? How about you, Lizzie? What did you dream?"

"I didn't have any dreams last night," Lizzie said. "But I did have an idea. It seems that Roger is having the same trouble with the Cranes that I had with Agnes and Molly. Maybe if he could make them feel more needed they would feel better about him helping them."

"They could help him with his homework," Buck said. "Everybody could use help with that. And then they'd feel needed."

"It's a possibility," Victoria said. "But I don't think Mr. Dale wants the people we're working with to be doing our schoolwork. And I still wonder what Gina's dream about the tournament has to do with this."

"Nothing at all," I said sharply. "Why don't you give up on the dreams, Victoria?"

"We could invite the Cranes to the tournament," Lizzie said. "Maybe we could tell them the Echoes need people to cheer them on and . . ."

"That's it!" Victoria gave a little shout and her curly head began to bob. "That's just what we need. Team spirit that involves the whole team, not just the Echoes but all of the people I'm working with on this project. I can't believe I thought of this."

"Lizzie thought of it," I said.

"She helped. And your dream helped. Didn't I tell you it would? I think the chairs were trying to tell me we'd need extra chairs at the tournament. Wait till Mr. Dale hears this. I'll get an A for sure. England, here I come!" And without another word to Buck, Lizzie, or me, Victoria took off down the hall.

I looked at Lizzie. She was staring after Victoria in bewilderment. So was Buck.

"Do you get what the idea is?" Buck asked.

"I think it has something to do with the Cranes' feeling needed because they're going to the tournament," Lizzie said. "But didn't Roger say Mrs. Crane was in a wheelchair? Maybe she won't want to go to any tournament."

"There weren't any wheelchairs in my dream," I said. "And that's not what they meant anyway."

Then I told Lizzie and Buck about the dribble drill I'd done with my father. "That's why I dreamed about chairs," I said. "No matter what Victoria says. Anyway, it's *my* dream. How can she tell me what my dream means? Can you believe she's such a know-it-all?"

"And having the Cranes come to the tournament was *my* idea," Lizzie said angrily. "I can't believe how she takes all the credit for it. What kind of a person would do that?"

"An obnoxious one," I said. I could feel my anger growing, and as Buck started to put his bag of peanut candy away I reached out and said, "Can I have a couple? I'm starving."

"Sure," Buck said. He poured a generous pile into my outstretched hand and as he did I realized he hadn't said a word about what had just happened.

"So what do you think, Buck?" I asked. "Isn't that pretty rotten of Victoria to take Lizzie's idea and act like it was hers? And how can she tell me what my dreams mean?"

Buck shrugged, and he did look really puzzled. "I don't know," he said. "I don't know anybody else that could do it. But maybe Victoria's some kind of genius."

Buck was *not* kidding. Buck was serious. "Victoria Chubb a genius?" I cried.

"Well, think about it," Buck began. But just then the warning bell rang. "I've got to go," he said. "I need a drink. Those peanuts made me thirsty. But think about it," he called over his shoulder as he started off.

I looked at Lizzie and shook my head. "I will not think about it," I said. "There is no way I will even consider that Victoria Chubb might be a genius!"

10

"**I**f Victoria Chubb is such a genius maybe she'll know what is supposed to be growing in this cup," I grumbled, as Lizzie and I slumped into our seats on the bus at the end of the day. Ms. Bugenhagen had passed out the mysterious seeds that afternoon. She gave each one of us a cup. In the bottom of each cup were several small seeds. Since each person had a different kind of seed the cups were numbered.

"Don't forget your number in case you want to plant your seeds in another container," Ms. Bugenhagen warned us. "I've got it all coded so I know who got which seeds. Good luck, everyone."

I looked at the hard, tiny, round seeds that were rolling about on the bottom of my white Styrofoam cup. I remembered Ms. Bugenhagen's words to us. "Through methods of observation, experimentation, and deduction, you will be able to identify the plants you'll grow," she'd said. Then we had to write a two-page report on our plant.

"Do these look like any seeds you know?" I asked Lizzie. She was about the smartest kid I knew. If Lizzie didn't know, nobody would.

"I don't know seeds, except grass seeds," Lizzie said. "And those aren't grass seeds. Every year my dad plants thousands of grass seeds and every year nothing grows."

"Why?" I asked. If thousands of grass seeds wouldn't grow for Lizzie's father, who was a pretty famous lawyer, how could Ms. Bugenhagen expect these seeds to grow for me?

"It has something to do with our soil," Lizzie said. "And with the tree roots that are too close to the surface. And with Sniper digging up holes all over the yard." Sniper is Lizzie's collie. Since I've known Lizzie he's not only dug up the yard, but also ripped up two of her mother's living room rugs.

"Well if nothing grows it's not going to be my fault," I said. "I hope my mother has some potting soil at home. If these seeds don't grow I don't know what I'm going to do. This project is one-fourth of our grade."

"Maybe you should fertilize them, too," Lizzie suggested as she got up to get off the bus. "I'll talk to you later."

"There's potting soil in the garage," my mother told me when I explained the project to her. "The kitchen window gets a lot of good sun. And it's high enough so you won't have to worry about Lester getting at it."

We didn't have any fertilizer so I just pushed the seeds into the soil and set the cup up on the windowsill.

"Have you mentioned going out for a birthday dinner to any of your friends?" my mother asked me as I poured water onto the soil. The little seeds came floating up to the top and I poked them under as the water disappeared into the soil.

"I've asked them all," I said. "Lizzie can't wait, Buck wanted to know if he could order whatever he wanted, and Roger said he'd go as long as Buck was going. But if Buck didn't go, he wouldn't go with just Lizzie and me."

"That's very honest of him," my mother said with a smile.

"Are you sure you don't know what kind of seeds these are?" I asked my mother.

"Positive," she said. "I'm not a gardener. Just wait until they grow. We won't know anything until then."

So from then on, except for watering them every couple of days, I didn't worry about them. Ms. Bugenhagen had told us it might take a while for some of the seeds to grow, so our reports weren't due until the end of the semester. After about ten days I did see tiny sprouts starting. They were pale green and didn't look like anything

I'd ever seen. "Give them time," my dad said. So that's what I did.

But if my seeds weren't developing much, my basketball team sure was. Every time I met with the Echoes it seemed they were better than the time before. "We practice after school every day," Timmy S. told me one afternoon just two weeks before the tournament.

"And at recess, too," Peter L. added. "And look what I have." He pointed to his glasses to show me the elastic strap that held them on. "My father said the real players wear these. He got them for me when I told him I was going to be in a tournament. Hey," he said, squinting through his glasses. "You look different."

Peter L. was right. I was wearing pink-and-white checked shorts with a pink-and-white striped T-shirt. I'd gotten new electric-pink high-tops as an early birthday gift and I had a pink headband with a white bow on it in my hair. I was tired of having to look so boring on the days I was coaching. And for the tournament I wanted to dress up — but still look like a coach.

"I like those sneakers," Timmy P. said.

"I don't," Eddie M. said.

I gave my whistle a sharp blow. "We don't have time to talk about clothes," I said. "Take your places on the court," I yelled, starting to dribble the ball toward the basket. "Today we'll start with

111

dribbling. Everyone gets a chance to dribble to the basket then take a shot. Just one shot. Then pass to the next guy. I want to practice your defense today, too."

"Me first," Timmy S. shouted.

"No, me first!" Peter G. cried. He gave Timmy S. a sharp jab with his elbow. Timmy S. yelled and turned to hit him. Peter G. saw the hit coming. He kicked Timmy S. in the shin. Timmy S. let out a loud cry.

This time when I blew my whistle it sounded as angry as I felt. The team wouldn't be able to do a thing if all they did was fight.

"Cut out the fighting!" I yelled, running up and getting between them to break up their squabble. "That's the first rule of being a team. Who knows how to spell team?" I asked.

"That's a cinch," Timmy P. said. "T-e-a-m."

"Right," I said. "So remember: In the word *team* there is no *I*. Get it?"

"No," Eddie M. and Peter L. said together.

"Think about it," I said. "Now Eddie K., you'll start the drill. Everyone else line up behind him."

"I get it!" Timmy P. shouted as they got into a line. "It means a team is everybody."

"Right," I said. "A team is everybody. Now everybody get going."

The practice was just about over when the door of the gym opened and in came Victoria Chubb. For a moment she stood and watched the practice.

I saw her sharp brown eyes lower to take in my electric-pink hightop sneakers. I saw them dart up to the white bow on my headband. Then I saw her make some sort of note on a clipboard she was carrying before she approached me and the Echoes.

"I have a couple of announcements," she said, setting her clipboard down on a chair in the corner of the gym before coming toward us. I was disappointed. The clipboard was so far away it would be impossible for me to see what she'd written. The boys stopped shooting.

"Who are you?" Eddie K. shouted.

"I am your team leader," Victoria said.

"What's that?" Eddie asked.

"It's like the principal," Victoria said. For a second the boys were quiet. They knew the principal was boss. But they knew Victoria was also just a kid.

"What's your name?" Peter G. asked.

"Ms. Chubb," Victoria said.

"Ms. Chubby?" Timmy S. echoed. He gave a little giggle.

"You can call me Victoria," Victoria said quickly. "And I'm not here to talk about me. I'm here to tell you about the tournament. It's been changed. Instead of being two weeks from Wednesday, it's two weeks from Friday."

"Oh no!" I said. I couldn't stop myself.

"What's the matter?" Victoria asked.

"That's my birthday," I said. Just last night my mother and I had made definite plans to get reservations for me and my friends for dinner at Tuesday's. I had picked Tuesday's because I'd gone there once for lunch with my mother. The food was delicious and there were tons of people, and I remembered thinking that a lot of them were dressed up and looked like they were on dates. It was exactly the sort of place I had wanted to go for my birthday.

"Friday is the only time we can get the gym," Victoria said. "The school team is playing an away game that night."

"Night!" I wailed. "Is the tournament going to be at night?"

"No," Victoria said. "It's going to be right after school. The kids will be brought over on a bus at three-thirty. Mr. Dale will pick up everyone else in the van. Of course, if you really can't make it, I could coach the team. I know a little bit about coaching myself."

"I can do it," I said quickly. There was no way I was going to let Victoria Chubb coach *my* team in the tournament.

"No problem then," Victoria said. "We'll be done by . . ."

Just then the gym door opened and Mr. Dale poked his head in. "Victoria, could I see you for a moment, please?"

Victoria hurried out of the gym, the boys picked

up where they were with the dribble practice, and I turned to watch them. As I did, I saw Victoria's clipboard still sitting on the chair in the corner. It couldn't hurt to go over and take a look at it, I figured. Besides, I was curious to know what she'd been writing when she looked at me. As the boys dribbled away again, I walked over and picked it up.

It was part of her team leader report. Apparently she had to do a report on everyone on the team because the first page said TEAM MEMBER and next to it she had written my name. Although I knew I shouldn't, I started to read it. *Gina Lazzaro is a nice person*, Victoria had written. *I had to help her find the job she would be best at. I had to tell her that her clothes are too flashy.* (This sentence Victoria had underlined twice.) *I helped her get her team in shape. I have come up with the idea of a tournament for all three teams. I have done everything I could to make her job better.*

For a second I couldn't believe what I was reading. There was not a word about what *I* had done. It was as if Victoria were coaching the team!

Quickly I flipped to the next member's report. It was Buck's. *Edward Buckley is a very nice person*, Victoria had written again. *I got him to do the tutoring by thinking of creative ways for him to teach. I gave him all my old* Teen Years *magazines. I also gave him all my mother's old nail polish. I helped him and encouraged him to do a good job.*

Quickly I flipped to the reports on Lizzie and Roger. Once again, Victoria took all the credit. It seemed as if she were doing everything and we were doing nothing. According to these reports, if it weren't for her the whole project would have been a flop.

"It's my turn. He pushed ahead of me!" Eddie K. and Peter L. had started to fight about whose turn it was to dribble. "I get the ball now!"

All at once I felt furious — furious at Victoria for what she'd written, and furious at the Echoes, for not taking turns. *"In the word* team *there is no* I!" I yelled at them. I wished Victoria were there to hear it, and suddenly, without thinking, I took the pen she had lying on the clipboard, and at the bottom of her report on me I wrote, *The motto of the Echoes is: In the word* team *there is no* I! *Think about it.*

Although I knew I had no right even to look at Victoria's report, much less to write on it, I couldn't help myself. I put the pen on the clipboard, and walked back onto the court.

"You actually wrote on Victoria's report?" Lizzie asked me. She had come to my house after school and we were in my room eating microwave popcorn with sour cream-and-chives topping.

"I couldn't help it," I said. "It made me sick!

We're the ones doing all the work and *she's* taking all the credit. What do you think she'll do?"

"I don't know," Lizzie said. "How will she know you wrote it?"

"Who else could it be?" I asked. "She only left her clipboard in the gym for a few minutes, and when she ran in to pick it up I was the only person around that could have done it. None of the Echoes would have. And we were the only people there."

"So she knows you read the reports, too," Lizzie said. "She's not going to like that."

I started to get a sick feeling. I knew what I'd done was wrong. "What if Victoria shows it to Mr. Dale? What if she takes it to Mr. Ramstead? What if, after all my work with the Echoes, she kicks me off the project?" I asked Lizzie. On the sports news on TV coaches are always being fired.

"I bet she won't," Lizzie said. But she didn't sound too convinced. This was one time when Lizzie, who could usually make me see things in a brighter light, couldn't help me at all.

"Gina!" My mother called me from downstairs. "Phone for you."

"Who is it?" I yelled.

"Victoria Chubb," my mother said. "She says it's important."

"Oh no," I whispered to Lizzie as I got up. "Can I use the phone in your room?" I yelled down to my mother.

"Don't be on too long," she called up to me.

Lizzie followed me into my parents' room. She sat on the edge of the bed next to me as I lifted the receiver. "Hello?" I said.

"Gina, this is Victoria. I just want to say a couple of things." From the sound of Victoria's voice I couldn't tell if she was angry or not.

"What?" I asked.

"I was wondering if the night of the tournament you'd like to come with the rest of the team to a cookout at my house. It won't really be a cookout, it will be a cook-in — because we have this gas grill in the kitchen that you can use all year."

"That sounds very nice, but . . ." Before I could go on, Victoria started talking.

"You see, as team leader I thought it might be a nice idea for the whole team to be together on that night. It will be the end of the project. I thought it would be good if we could all get together to sort of celebrate."

"I'm afraid I already have plans," I said. Hadn't I told Victoria that Friday was my birthday? Didn't she figure I might be doing something special?

But I was relieved. Either Victoria didn't know I was the one who'd written on her report, or she didn't care.

"I hope you won't mind if I go and ask Buck, Lizzie, and Roger then," she went on. "Even though it won't be the whole team I'd like to have some of us together that night."

I felt a nervous twitter in my throat. I swallowed. "Buck, Lizzie, and Roger have plans, too," I said. My voice sounded a little squeaky. Why did I let Victoria Chubb make me so nervous? Beside me on the bed Lizzie gave me a poke and a baffled look.

"Are you sure?" Victoria asked.

"Yes," I said. "They're going with me. It's my birthday and my parents said I could invite a group of my friends to go out to dinner with me. We're going to Tuesday's."

The minute I'd let it out, I knew I was doomed. This was what always happened when I got around Victoria. I got so confused I ended up telling her too much.

"You mean the whole team will be going to Tuesday's on Friday night after the game?" she asked.

Suddenly Victoria's voice sounded a little shaky. I thought she might be going to cry. And I knew if she did, it would be my fault. After all, she'd called to invite our team to a cookout, only to find out we already had a party planned — and she wasn't invited.

"Not the team exactly . . ." I started to say.

"Buck, Lizzie, Roger, and you," Victoria interrupted. "That's my whole team, isn't it?"

"I guess it is," I said weakly. There was a moment of silence. I thought I heard a sniff. "Well, I suppose my parents wouldn't mind if you came, too," I finally said. I heard Lizzie gasp.

"That would be great," Victoria said. Her voice was back to normal. "What time are you going?" she asked. "And what is everybody wearing? I mean, Tuesday's is sort of dressy, isn't it?"

"We are going to get dressed up," I said weakly. "We're meeting at my house around seven." I couldn't look at Lizzie. I knew what she must be thinking. Because I was thinking the same thing. What kind of jerk was I anyway? I didn't want Victoria Chubb at my birthday dinner. And yet I had just heard myself invite her. How had that happened?

"Sounds super," Victoria said enthusiastically. "And Gina, the other thing I wanted to tell you was that I like that motto you gave the Echoes."

"Motto?" I said.

"You know, the one you wrote on the clipboard. I'm going to try and work it into my report somehow. 'In the word *team* there is no *I*.' I really like that a lot."

"I'm glad you like it," I said.

Then Victoria and I hung up. I looked at Lizzie. She was shaking her head and from the look on her face I couldn't tell if she was laughing or ready to cry.

"I don't believe it!" she shouted. "Did I just

hear you invite Victoria Chubb to your birthday?"

"She made me," I said weakly. "I don't know exactly how, but she made me invite her."

Lizzie scowled. "How could she make you?"

"You know how," I said sharply. "The same way she made us do the Creative Social Studies Project. It wasn't really my fault."

I guess Lizzie could tell I was getting upset. "Maybe your mother won't let her come," she suggested.

But my mother was no help. "If you've already invited her, you can't very well take back the invitation," she said, when we ran down to ask her. "But don't invite anyone else. Four friends are enough."

I turned away so my mother wouldn't see the miserable look on my face. I felt like crying. My birthday was ruined — all because I couldn't keep my mouth shut. "I'm not having four friends at my party," I grumbled. "I'm having three friends — three friends and one Victoria Chubb."

11

"So what did the Cranes say when you invited them to the tournament?" I asked Roger. It was the Wednesday before the tournament — and before my birthday — and I spotted him leaving to go to the Cranes' house as I headed to the gym to meet the Echoes. Even though it had only been a few days since I'd last seen Roger, he seemed even taller than before.

"I think they're coming," Roger said. He sounded a little uncertain. "It wasn't easy to convince them. I practically had to beg Mrs. Crane. First I told them we really needed people to come and cheer the team on. They didn't seem too interested. But when I told them how hard everyone was working they finally agreed to give it a try. And I guess their grandson in California used to play basketball in high school and they went to all his games. I think they miss having young people around."

"Is Mr. Dale going to pick them up?" I asked.

"No, we're getting the seniors' van. I don't

know if Mrs. Crane's too happy about it. She's been sort of quiet the last few times I've been there. Do you know, she hasn't been out of the house in almost two years?"

"Maybe it will be good for them," I said.

"I hope so," Roger said. "I think they were a little embarrassed when I told them about the seniors' van. I don't think they even knew it existed."

How could someone not know about the seniors' van? I wondered. It was a big old school bus painted glossy white, and in huge red letters it said SENIORS ON THE MOVE. I saw it around town all the time.

"But Gina," Roger went on, and his voice got louder with excitement. "You should see Mr. Crane's train set. It's gigantic. I've never seen anything like it. I want my dad to go over, and Buck wants to see it, and when Tommy comes home for vacation I'm taking him there, too."

Stupidly I asked, "Is it big enough so you can ride in it?"

Roger looked at me as if I were about six years old. "Not that kind of gigantic, Gina," he said with exaggerated patience. "I mean Mr. Crane has miles of track running all around his basement. You can stand in the middle and work the controls and this train will go anywhere you want it to, up mountains, over bridges, through tunnels. And it makes station stops in little towns. I'm telling you, it's unbelievable."

"It sounds good," I said, trying to appreciate it like Roger did.

"It's beyond good," Roger said. "Way, way, way beyond good." Then he looked a little embarrassed. "Those are neat earrings, Gina," he said. "Where'd you get them?"

"Thanks," I said. The earrings were new. I was surprised Roger had noticed them. They were in the shape of candles, with the flame sparkling on my earlobe and the candle and holder dangling almost to my shoulder. "I got them at Wing-it, the new store in the mall. Maybe your mom would like a pair."

"Yea," Roger said.

"So are you all set for dinner at Tuesday's Friday night?" I asked him.

"Yea," he said. For a second he looked a little uneasy. "Buck's going, right?" he asked.

"Buck's going," I said. I didn't mention how I had been forced into inviting Victoria Chubb. I knew Roger was a little shy about going out to dinner with girls and I didn't want to scare him off.

"It should be great. My mother says we can order anything we want, including dessert, even though she's sending over cake from Artillo's Bakery. And after dinner I might get a video so we can go back to my house and watch it while we finish off what's left of the cake."

"If you see the *North by Northwest* video get

that," Roger said. "Mr. Crane told me it has a great train scene in it. I was going to get it for us to watch together but the Cranes don't have a VCR."

As I headed for the gym I couldn't help but think that it sounded as if Roger and the Cranes had gotten to be pretty close friends. Which meant that once again, Victoria and her project were looking good — even though the truth was she had very little to do with it.

"Timmy S. has the chicken pox!" That was the news that greeted me when I entered the gym that afternoon, two days before the tournament.

"Timmy S!" I cried. Timmy S. was the closest thing I had to a star player. He was the tallest of the six boys, and if anyone was likely to make a basket, it was him.

"Yep," Eddie K. said. "His dad came to school today and got his work for the week. He can't be in the tournament."

I could see by the boys' faces that they were upset. But as coach I knew I had to act as if I weren't.

"Timmy S. is a very good player," I told them. "But you're all good. This just means there won't be anyone on the bench. We'll need all five players on the court at all times."

"Do you think we can win?" Peter G. asked me.

"I think you have as good a chance as anyone,"

I said. "We may have to work a little harder but we'll play our best, we'll have fun, and we'll try to win. Now get in line and we'll practice your passing."

As I watched my team line up I felt proud. In their bright yellow pinnies with their names written on the back, they looked cute. And they were so serious about the game. Even though their legs were short, they were willing to try — to jump for the basket, to run around the net, to get into better positions. I realized I didn't really care that much if they won or lost the game. I just wanted people to see them play.

My first thought when I woke up Friday morning was, Today is my birthday! My second thought was, Today is the tournament. My third thought was, Tonight I'll be having dinner at Tuesday's. My fourth thought was, Let's get this day going — and I leapt out of bed!

Next to my place at the breakfast table my parents had left an envelope. Inside was a card with a vase of red and yellow tulips on the front. When I opened it I read: *Your reservation at Tuesday's is for seven-thirty tonight. Happy thirteenth birthday!*

"Thanks Mom," I said. My dad had already left for work and my mother was feeding Lester as I sat down to a blueberry muffin and juice.

"Don't let me forget to give you the credit card

before you leave tonight," my mother said. "I've already told Tuesday's you have our permission to use it."

"I can't wait," I said. "I just hope Victoria Chubb doesn't ruin things."

"How could she?" my mother asked. "It's your birthday, your friends. Just ignore her if she starts to get difficult."

I didn't want to argue with my mother after all she'd done to make this birthday special for me. But Victoria Chubb was not an easy person to ignore.

At school that day I couldn't wait for the time to pass. But each time I looked, the hands on the clock seemed stuck. Lunchtime finally came, then study hall, English during last period, and finally I found myself heading down to meet my team.

In the gym, one section of bleachers had been opened up. I saw Lizzie and Roger talking to an elderly man who was standing beside a woman in a wheelchair — Mrs. and Mr. Crane — and two women who were carrying long white, red-tipped canes — Lizzie motioned for me to join them.

"This is my friend, Gina Lazzaro," Lizzie said, introducing me to Molly and Agnes. "She's the coach for the Echoes."

"And this is Mr. and Mrs. Crane," Roger said, smiling at the woman in the wheelchair and the tall, thin, gray-haired man who stood beside her.

"We've heard a lot about your team." Mr. Crane

reached out his hand to give mine a firm shake. "Roger's been telling us how hard you've worked. In our day no girl would ever have coached a basketball team. But things sure have changed." Mr. Crane gave Roger an admiring look. "And thanks to Roger here, we've learned about some of the changes that can help us out. Do you know we didn't even realize there was a seniors' van in town until Roger told us about it?" Roger didn't say anything, but he sure looked pleased.

Across the gym, Buck was with some guys from his homeroom. But he was doing what I was doing, keeping one eye on the door. So far the bus that brought the little kids up from the elementary school hadn't arrived.

A few minutes later a group of little kids walked in, including Ellissa and Tracey. They waved to me but ran over to Buck. To my surprise they gave him big hugs, which Buck happily returned. Then he pointed to a space on the bleachers and they went and sat down. I was amazed at how well he'd gotten them to behave.

Pretty soon a group of six boys came in, dressed to play basketball. For the first time I was seeing a rival team. I sized up the boys as they headed toward Bob Zacarro, the coach from Henry Richter's group. He was yelling "All Rangers, over here! Get your pinnies on." The boys didn't look much taller than my team, and I noticed they tried to push ahead of each other as Bob passed out their bright red pinnies. Not a good sign of team-work, I thought.

I watched as Bob huddled with them, then handed one of them a basketball and sent them onto the court to warm up. Watching them dribble the ball I relaxed a little. They didn't have as much control as my guys did, that was for sure.

Over on the other side of the gym, Reggie Green was giving his team a pep talk before sending them out to warm up. I could hear it from where I stood, as could everyone else in the gym. His group leader, Tammi Chen, was nodding happily, and I could see why. I didn't know Reggie was one of the coaches and my stomach felt slushy as I listened to him.

"You guys know what I expect," he was saying sternly. "I expect to be proud of you. I expect you're gonna show this room how to play basketball."

Clustered around Reggie Green, the heads of six small boys nodded obediently. On each of their green pinnies someone had drawn the face of an angry bull. The boys looked up at Reggie in awe, and it was no wonder. Reggie Green was almost six feet tall. He was thin, lean, and as he talked one long, dark arm casually bounced a basketball, with the same ease I would tap my foot. My stomach went from slush to turmoil as I heard Reggie's last directions to his guys. "Knock 'em off the court!" he cried as his team headed out to warmup.

There were now two teams warming up on the court. And one team missing. The Echoes were nowhere to be seen. I felt a crazy panic come over me as I kept staring at the gym door waiting for them to come in. But no one appeared. What if they all had chicken pox? I wondered wildly. But wouldn't someone have told me? Or maybe they just got too scared at the last minute. Could they still be out on the bus? Had I coached them so badly they were afraid to face another team?

I caught Lizzie's eye as she talked to Agnes. She gave me a puzzled frown. I shrugged and she came over to me. "Where's your team?"

"I don't know," I said. "They should be here. All the kids come in on the same bus."

"You'd better find Victoria then. Something's going on. And your team is missing out on the warm-up. That's not fair."

I knew Lizzie was right. I had to find Victoria. But that was another problem. She was nowhere to be seen either. What was going on? All the other leaders were here, why wasn't she? I tried to remember if I'd seen her at all that day. Maybe she was absent. Then I remembered I had seen her going into the cafeteria at lunchtime. She had waved and I had sort of waved, then looked the other way.

Nervously I looked around the gym. The crowd, which was made up of all sorts of people with whom the Creative Social Studies Project had worked, was starting to settle down. They wanted to start the game.

"I'm going to go look for them," I said.

"I'd better go back to Agnes and Molly," Lizzie said. "Let me know if anything's wrong."

She turned to go back to her seat and I started for the door. I didn't know where I was going to look. I thought I could check the bus. Then maybe I could find Mr. Dale. He might know what was happening. I stepped outside the gym and looked up and down the hall. Then I spotted them. Victoria and the Echoes were racing down the hall. Victoria's leather briefcase was flapping at her side. The boys, wearing new yellow T-shirts, were flushed with excitement.

"Aren't these T-shirts neat?" Peter G. cried. "Victoria got them for us." The T-shirts were yellow with two black mountains and the words THE ECHOES printed on them. But I didn't care about the T-shirts. I cared about the game.

"What's going on!" I shouted. I was mad. "Don't you know we've got a game to play? You're missing the warm-up! Don't blame me if you lose, because this is all your fault."

Five sets of eyes looked at me in shame. "Sorry, coach," Eddie K. said, as I hurried them into the gym.

"The Echoes and I had a little business to attend to," Victoria said, as if it didn't matter at all that my team was missing valuable practice time.

"They're ready to play now." I didn't even look at her as my team headed for the court.

For about two minutes the Echoes joined the other teams on the floor and warmed up. I shouted directions to them, but I wasn't happy with the way they looked. They seemed stiff and they kept stopping to check out the people in the audience. Then Mr. Dale stepped onto the court and the teams went to their coaches as he explained how the tournament would be played.

"Good afternoon ladies and gentlemen," Mr. Dale said. "This afternoon I am both happy and a little sad. I am happy to see what a great turnout we have — and to congratulate everyone on a very successful Creative Social Studies Project." There was a burst of loud applause. "But I am sad because this is our last meeting."

I looked at my friends. Buck, Lizzie, and Roger looked pleased, and I was, too. In spite of Victoria Chubb, I think we were all glad we'd done it.

"One of our team leaders, Victoria Chubb, came up with this idea for a tournament." Mr. Dale turned to find Victoria in the crowd. She stood up and waved. There was a scattering of polite applause.

"Since we have three teams, which is a bit inconvenient, we'll have to have two shortened games. I'll draw a name from the hat to see which team will play the winners of the first game." Mr. Dale reached into a hat he was holding and pulled out a small slip of paper. "The Echoes," he announced. "So the Bulls and the Rangers will play first, and the Echoes will play the winners."

That was a relief. At least the Echoes would have a chance to watch the other teams in action. But once their game had begun, my feeling of relief didn't last long. The Bulls quickly took possession of the ball, and before the Rangers could even figure out which basket was theirs, the Bulls had scored four points. Reggie Green was jumping up and down shouting, "Way to go, Bulls! Show 'em what you've got!"

Bob Zacarro called for time-out. His team ran over to him and I could see him gesturing wildly. The Echoes gave me worried looks. I couldn't meet their eyes. The whistle blew and play resumed.

In the second quarter, the Rangers finally made a basket. Bob Zacarro screamed and clapped. So did most of the audience, in sympathy. But as the Rangers were smiling at each other over their two points, the Bulls scored four more.

By the fourth quarter it was eighteen to ten and the Bulls were confident. They tossed the ball back and forth, teasing the Rangers, who just weren't quick enough to get it back. One of the Rangers stuck his tongue out at a Bull. That made the Bulls mad and they quickly made another basket just as time ran out.

Mr. Dale blew his whistle. "Congratulations to

the Bulls and great playing by the Rangers. Fifteen minutes to rest and the Bulls take on the Echoes."

I thought I might throw up. Each of the Echoes looked as scared to death as I felt. But I was the coach. I could not show my fear. "All right, men," I said. I had never called them men before. But it sounded stronger than *guys*. "The Bulls are the team to beat."

"Right, coach," said Eddie M. "They're good, aren't they?"

"Just as good as you," I said. "Now remember everything I've told you."

Peter L. looked seriously at his teammates from behind his thick glasses. "In the word *team* there is no *I*," he said.

"Right," I said. "Just remember that and you'll do fine."

With a feeling of dread I watched them bound out onto the court. Before the Echoes even realized the game had begun the Bulls snatched the ball and quickly made the first basket.

"Show 'em who's boss!" Reggie Green bellowed from the sidelines. His team turned to look at him. Peter G. took advantage of the distraction and grabbed the ball. He passed it to Eddie K. who dribbled it to the basket and took a shot. The ball bounced off the backboard, rolled slowly around the rim, and after wobbling for a moment, dropped in.

I went wild. "Great play!" I screamed. "Keep it up, Echoes!" I saw Lizzie stand up to clap. Buck gave a screeching whistle and Roger stomped his feet. Victoria Chubb had brought a party noisemaker, and she gave a long, loud toot on it. More people cheered. Even Mrs. Crane was clapping hard from her wheelchair.

But the crowd just made the Bulls play even harder. And by the third quarter they were ahead, twelve to six. The Echoes were looking bewildered. I called for a time-out.

The Echoes clustered around me. "Look," I said. "Don't let them scare you. Help each other get the ball to the basket. You can do it!"

And the Echoes did. So did the Bulls. But by the last minute of the game, the Echoes had tied it up, eighteen all. Now Reggie called a time-out. I tried to cheer up the Echoes, but they were getting pretty worn out. Reggie huddled his team and whispered to them. They returned to the court smiling as the Echoes gave each other, and me, worried looks.

For the first few seconds of play the Echoes held onto the ball. Then a Bull took possession. He passed it to another Bull, who shot it way up the court to where another Bull was waiting. And he made a basket, just as Mr. Dale blew the whistle signaling the game was over.

The Bulls — and the crowd — went crazy with joy. I clapped hard, too, although I was a little disappointed. But eighteen to twenty was a nice score, I told myself. We had nothing to be ashamed of.

I watched as my team shook hands with the Bulls and then started toward me. Just then Mr. Dale came onto the floor again. "Great playing by everyone," he exclaimed. "Congratulations to all three teams and to their coaches, but especially to our champions, the Bulls." The Bulls let out a noisy roar. "And I have trophies for *all* our players.

"And now," Mr. Dale went on, "one of our team leaders would like to say a few words."

I turned around just in time to see Victoria Chubb heading for the center of the floor. She smiled at the crowd. "Today has been great," she said. "I know how hard the team leaders worked to make this project a success and I can see we did it."

Naturally, I thought, she has to get in a good word for the team leaders. But why was she bothering, I wondered? Mr. Dale looked so happy I was sure he was going to give us all A's.

"Today is not only the last day of the project, it is also someone's birthday," Victoria went on, looking right at me. I could feel my neck turning warm, and my cheeks burning.

"Because she has been such a good coach, the guys on her team would like to give her a gift and some cards. Gina Lazzaro, will you please come up here!"

The crowd began to clap as I walked toward Victoria. She waved to the Echoes and they came up, too. Each one of them had a card for me, and Victoria handed me a box. Quickly, with shaking hands, I unwrapped it. It was a purple scarf with threads of silver and gold running through it. I had admired one just like it at Wing-it last week.

"Thank you," I said, giving each of the boys a hug, as they each gave me a handmade card. "You're a wonderful team."

"That's why we were late for the warm-up," Eddie M. said. "Victoria wanted us all to make you a card."

"Thanks, Victoria," I said. I hoped I sounded like I meant it. But that was the trouble with Victoria Chubb. She could get you all confused.

Minutes later, as we filed out of the gym, I was still trying to figure her out. Then the words from an old nursery rhyme suddenly popped into my head. I could remember my mom saying this about me when I was around four years old: "When she was good, she was very, very, good," she'd say. "But when she was bad, she was horrid."

12

"We lost, but we played really well," I told my mother as I rushed into the kitchen at five-thirty that evening. I had gotten a ride home with Roger's mother after the tournament, but I was feeling rushed. Our reservations were at seven-thirty and I still had to take a bath, wash my hair, do my nails, and decide what to wear.

"What was the score?" my mother asked, taking the dustpan away from Lester, who was crawling around on the kitchen floor, and replacing it with an old dented pan.

"Eighteen to twenty," I said. "The Rangers got clobbered by the Bulls but the Echoes fought back pretty well. Actually, it was a good game. And look what they gave me," I said, pulling the purple scarf and cards from my purse.

"Nice scarf," my mother said. "I can't believe fourth-grade boys could pick out such a lovely gift."

"Well, they had a little help," I said.

"Did Lizzie help them?" my mother asked.

138

"Victoria Chubb did," I said. I didn't look directly at my mother. I knew what she would say, and sure enough, she said it.

"Now aren't you glad you invited Victoria to your party, Gina? She must like you a lot to do something so thoughtful."

"She might like me a little, but knowing Victoria Chubb she only did it to make herself look good," I told my mother. "She would have done anything to get an A in social studies so she could go to England with her father." I grabbed a handful of peanuts from a bowl on the counter, and as I did I took a quick look at my seeds again. They had started to grow a couple of days ago. The little sprouts had turned into green leaves. But they didn't look like any leaves I'd ever seen before. My mother didn't know what they were either. Now I picked one off. It had a strong funny smell that reminded me of pepper. And the leaves were growing rounded along the edges like little hearts.

"I still have no idea what they are," I said, grabbing more peanuts. "And right now I don't even care."

My mother smiled. "Don't ruin your appetite," she warned me as I started upstairs. "There're some cards and a small gift on your bed."

My grandparents in Florida had sent me a pretty card, with a check for twenty dollars inside. My aunt and uncle in Phoenix had sent me a twenty-five-dollar savings bond. And from Lester there was a paperback book called *Knowing Plants — The Complete Guide to Whatever Grows*. (I had a feeling he'd had some help selecting it.) I flipped through the book and saw hundreds of pictures of plants. All I'd have to do was find in the book what was growing in my Styrofoam cup and do my report. Of course, since I'd have to study hundreds of pictures of plants it would take some time. But at least I had something to go on. Anyway, I wasn't going to worry about that foolish plant now.

I raced back downstairs. "Thanks, Lester," I said. "Great gift. You're a very smart little kid." I leaned down and gave him a hug, but Lester just grinned at me and kept on banging his pan on the kitchen floor. "Thanks, Mom," I called, as I started upstairs again to take my bath.

By the time my parents finished their dinner at six-thirty, I was just about ready. I had put on four different outfits and changed my mind four different times. As hostess I thought I should be the most dressed up, so I finally chose a black velvet skirt I'd worn last year at Christmas, and a fluffy white sweater. It looked too plain, so I took the scarf the Echoes had given me and wrapped that around my neck. Then I took a rhinestone pin my mother had given me from her old jewelry box and pinned that on the scarf. Against the gold-and-silver threads it looked perfect.

Since the scarf was purple I pulled out my purple tights and dressy black shoes, but to be sure I didn't look too gaudy I wore my tiniest gold earrings.

"You look wonderful!" my father said when I came into the kitchen a few minutes later. "Now how's this going to work? I'll drop you off at seven-thirty and do you want me to come back around nine or do you want to call me when you're ready?"

"I'll call," I said.

"Take some change," my mother reminded me. "And while I think of it, here's the credit card. Don't lose it."

"Don't worry, Mom," I said. But a little tingle of nervous excitement ran through me as I took the card and carefully zippered it into a small compartment inside my purse.

By seven-fifteen Roger, Lizzie, and Buck were there. Everybody looked great. Lizzie had on a pink dress with lace around the collar, pink flats, and a big pink ribbon pulling her long hair into a ponytail off to one side.

Roger had on a blue-and-white striped shirt, blue pants, and new penny loafers that looked almost as shiny as his face as he handed me my gift. "Happy birthday," he mumbled a little awkwardly.

I unwrapped the small box. It was from Wing-it and when I opened it I found a pair of earrings. They were like my candle earrings that Roger had admired on Wednesday, only instead of candles these were triple-scoop ice-cream cones. The vanilla scoop rested on my ear lobe, while the chocolate and strawberry scoops and the cone hung below.

"If you don't like them you can take them back," Roger said.

"I love them," I told him. And, because he didn't seem totally convinced, I took out the small gold ones I was wearing and put on the ice-cream cones. They didn't exactly go with my outfit, but it seemed to make Roger happy.

"Nice tie," he teased Buck.

"I'm taking it off, don't worry," Buck said. He glared at Roger. "I only wore it because my mother made me." The tie was red-and-black striped and it looked very nice on Buck, who had on a white shirt, black pants, and a black-and-white checked sports coat. He yanked the tie off. "If Roger doesn't have to walk around being strangled tonight neither do I," he said.

Then he reached into his jacket pocket. "Here, Gina," he said. "Happy birthday."

Buck's gift was a ceramic pin. By perfect coincidence it was of three purple pansies in a tiny bouquet. "I think I'll wear this, too," I said, taking off the rhinestone I'd pinned on the scarf and replacing it with the pansies. It didn't seem fair to put on Roger's earrings and not also wear Buck's pin.

Lizzie's box was bigger. I unwrapped it to find a long flannel nightgown. It had a picture of a yawning cat on the front and his whiskers were two long feathers stitched onto the material. "It's beautiful," I said.

"Nice," Roger muttered.

"Who wants feathers when they're sleeping?" Buck asked.

"Everyone," Lizzie said. "Ever hear of down pillows and quilts, Buck? They're filled with feathers."

Buck knew Lizzie was right, so he didn't argue. Instead he said, "Well, now that you've got the loot, Gina, are we ready to eat?"

I looked at the clock on the mantel. It said seven-twenty. I knew I had told everyone to be there at seven. And everyone was — except Victoria. "We're sort of waiting for someone," I said.

"Who?" Roger asked.

Just then my dad and mom came in. "Everybody ready?" My dad was dangling his car keys.

"Victoria Chubb isn't here yet," I said.

"*Who?*" Roger asked.

"Victoria Chubb," I said quietly. "I had to ask her. I didn't really want to but I had to." I saw my mother giving me a warning look. I knew I wasn't being polite, but I was starting to get mad. Everyone else had come on time. Now, not only had Victoria forced her way into my dinner, she was holding everything up. It wasn't fair.

Roger made a face. "I didn't know she was coming," he said. "Did you, Buck?"

Buck shrugged. "Nope." But he didn't seem to mind too much.

"Do you think you should call her?" my mother asked. "Maybe she forgot."

"I'll call," I said. I was glad for something to do. I felt uncomfortable standing around waiting. I went to the kitchen phone book, found the Chubb's number and dialed. The phone rang and rang about ten times. There was no answer.

I went back into the living room. "There's no answer," I said.

"Maybe she's on her way," my mother suggested.

A low rumble came from Buck's direction. He grabbed his stomach, laughing. "I only had two bagels with cream cheese when I got home from school today," he said. "I'm starving."

"Listen," my mother said. "Why don't you all start over to Tuesday's. When Victoria gets here I can drive her . . ."

But just then the doorbell rang and it was Victoria. "Sorry I'm late," she said breathlessly. "There was a little confusion. My father thought my mother was taking me but my mother had an emergency business meeting at the last minute and the housekeeper was gone for the day and so I didn't have any way to get here. So I called my mother out of the meeting and started yelling at

144

her and she called me a cab. But the cab took forever to get to my house. But it finally got there."

Victoria rattled this all off as the rest of us stood looking at her. And she did look great. As she unbuttoned her coat I could see she had on a black velvet dress with gray satin on the collar and waist. Around her neck was a pearl necklace and she had pearl earrings and a bracelet to match. Her black shoes had tiny heels on them, and her stockings were a glimmery gray. So much for the hostess being the most dressed up, I thought, as I got my coat.

"No problem," I heard my mother saying. "We're just glad you could come."

"Here, Gina," Victoria said, handing me a large blue envelope. "My mother was supposed to get you a gift but she didn't have much time."

"You gave her that lovely scarf," my mother said. "That was plenty."

"Right," I said as I opened the card. Suddenly I was glad I was wearing it. I felt a little sorry for Victoria. It didn't seem like she saw her parents too often. Maybe that was why she was so eager to go to England with her father.

The card had a big picture of a basketball on the front. On the front it read: *Hope this day is a ball for you*, and inside it said *Have a high-scoring birthday!* "Isn't that perfect?" Victoria said. "I just had to get it for you."

Inside also there was a folded piece of paper. I took it out and read it. It was a gift certificate to Wing-it for twenty-five dollars. I couldn't believe my eyes and I didn't know what to say. Luckily my mother spoke up.

"Victoria, this is most generous, but you really didn't have to get Gina anything else. The scarf was plenty."

"But this way Gina can get whatever she wants," Victoria said. "That's why my parents gave me a charge account at Wing-it. Now they don't have to bother going with me all the time. Or buying stuff that only gets returned. It's really much easier."

"Well, thank you," my mother said. I couldn't tell what she thought about the idea of a charge account. I'd have to ask her later. "Now you people better get going. Have fun."

We all piled into my dad's car and about ten minutes later he dropped us off in front of Tuesday's. Under the awnings over the big front windows you could see lights blazing and people moving about inside. As we all filed in I suddenly felt a little nervous. We were a few minutes late. And what was I supposed to say? But I didn't have to say anything.

Victoria led us to the desk where a young woman was checking coats. "Lazzaro, party of five," Victoria said. "We have a seven-thirty reservation."

"Would you like to check your coats?" the woman asked as she crossed something off in a big book.

"Yes," Victoria said, making the decision for all of us.

We handed our coats over to the woman who said, "Your table is ready. Kathleen, our hostess, will seat you in a moment."

We all stood around, waiting for Kathleen, not talking, just taking in the whole place. All around us were booths and tables, filled with elegantly dressed people eating dinner. Although it wasn't dark, the lights were low and on each table there was a candle.

As we were finally led to our table I felt very grown-up. People glanced up as we went by. I bet they were looking for the adult that was with us. I bet they were surprised to find there wasn't one.

"Your waitress will be with you in a minute," Kathleen told us as we took our seats. Lizzie and Roger sat next to me. Buck sat next to Roger and Victoria sat between Buck and Lizzie.

"Does anybody know what they're having?" Lizzie asked.

"One of everything," Buck said. Everyone laughed, especially Victoria. Buck looked pleased, and it was then I noticed he had put his tie back on.

"How come you put your tie back on?" I asked him.

"Yea, are you going to be able to swallow with

that thing around your neck?" Roger teased.

"I didn't want to lose it," Buck said. "It's my father's." But he looked a little embarrassed, and suddenly it occurred to me that maybe he had put it on because Victoria was there. But there wasn't time to think about that because our waitress, who turned out to be a waiter named Billy, was suddenly at the table asking us if we wanted anything from the bar.

"I'll have a Coke," I said. My mother had told me it was up to me to order first to put everyone at ease.

"Me, too." Lizzie said.

"Same," Roger said.

"Diet Coke," Buck ordered.

"And I'll have a ginger ale," Victoria said. "With a slice of orange, and a cherry. And do you have any of those little umbrellas that go on fruit drinks? I'd like one of those on it, too."

"Sure thing," Billy said.

He hurried away after handing each of us a menu. "These menus are almost as big as our math books," Roger said, leafing through the dozen or so pages of the tall menu. "I don't know what to have."

"Start with an appetizer," Victoria said. "I don't know if I'll have the escargots or a shrimp cocktail."

Lizzie gave her a cool look. "I don't know how anyone can eat escargots," she said.

148

"I don't know how anybody can say it," Buck said. "By the way, what is it?"

Even though I didn't want to admit it, I had no idea what escargots was either. Nor, I suspected, did Roger.

"They're snails," Victoria said matter-of-factly. We all groaned. "They're really very delicious. But I think I'll have a shrimp cocktail," she quickly added.

I got the feeling she was just showing off. I bet she didn't like the thought of eating snails anymore than the rest of us.

Billy returned with our drinks. Next to our four plain, little Cokes, Victoria's ginger ale really stood out. It was in a tall frosted glass, with two orange slices, two cherries, and a green-and-white dotted umbrella poking over the top.

We all grabbed for our Cokes the second Billy put them down. "Just a minute," Victoria called. She held up her glass. "I think we should have a toast. To Gina's birthday and to the great team I picked for the social studies project," she said.

That old saying, In the word *team* there is no *I*, flashed through my head. I felt like reminding her of it right then and there. But I didn't.

Instead we all clicked our glasses together. Even though I was having a good time, I couldn't help but feel that somehow Victoria Chubb was running *my* party.

"I'll have a small salad for my appetizer," I said. "What does everyone else want?"

"I'll have that, too," Lizzie said.

"I'm having minestrone soup," Buck said. "It's the soup of the day."

"I'll have onion soup," Roger said.

"Shrimp cocktail," Victoria said.

The soups and salads came in small bowls. The shrimp cocktail was on a large, fancy platter. It was lying on mounds of ice, surrounded by what looked like a whole head of lettuce. Next to the six fat, pink shrimps was a mound of sauce and several lemon slices. People at the table next to ours turned to watch who was getting it. I was sure Billy must have thought Victoria was the one having the birthday, not me.

When we were just about done with our appetizers, Billy came back to take our dinner order. Buck wanted the spaghetti. Roger ordered a steak, medium-well. Lizzie and I looked at each other. We couldn't make up our minds.

"I'll have the Five-Greens Salad," Victoria said. "But I don't think everyone is ready to order, so would you mind giving us a little more time?"

Even though I was annoyed that she sounded like a grown-up who'd eaten out a hundred times, I was glad for the few extra minutes to make my decision.

"What's the Five-Greens Salad?" I asked Victoria.

"Oh, it has all sorts of lettuce and greens in it," Victoria said. "My mother told me to order it so

I wouldn't be too filled up. That's what she does on all her business dinners."

I found the description of Victoria's salad on the menu, but it wasn't anything I'd want to eat for dinner. Half the stuff in it I'd never heard of.

"I think I'll have a steak, too," I told Billy when he returned. "Medium-rare."

"And I'll have spaghetti," Lizzie said.

"And could we have more rolls?" Buck asked.

"And butter. And water, please?" Victoria asked. "And our candle's gone out, too. Would you mind lighting it again?"

Billy smiled as he leaned over her to light the candle. But I got the feeling he was getting a little annoyed.

Soon our dinners were delivered. They looked, smelled, and tasted delicious. For a few moments no one spoke. We all just watched each other eat. I was watching Victoria. Her salad came in a huge glass bowl: leaves in all shades of green, with mushroom, tomatoes, and a bunch of other vegetables piled on top. All of a sudden I cried, "Don't eat that, Victoria!"

Victoria's fork froze before her mouth. "What's wrong with it?" she asked.

Everyone stopped eating to stare at me. "There's nothing wrong with it," I said. "But what is it?" I pointed to whatever it was that was hanging off the end of Victoria's fork.

"This?" Victoria said, pulling a long, smooth

green leaf off for me to look at. The edges of the leaf were rounded like little hearts. "It's roquette, I think."

"Row . . . what?" I asked. "Can I see it?"

"Here," Victoria said handing it over to me. "Yes, it's definitely roquette. I can tell by the smell. It's part of the mustard family. You can have it. I don't like it that much. They put it in the salad every night at investment camp. The chef called it *rocket* salad. Some of the kids liked it, but I always thought it tasted too bitter."

I took the long green leaf and looked at it carefully. I was sure it was the same as the leaves that were growing in my Styrofoam cup at home. I held it to my nose. It had the same strange smell. "This is what Ms. Bugenhagen has me growing," I said. "Boy, Victoria, am I ever glad you ordered that salad!"

Victoria beamed at me. "Isn't it a good thing I came?" she asked.

I popped the piece of roquette into my mouth. I wasn't crazy about its taste. But I figured I'd be better off with my mouth full. That way I wouldn't have to answer Victoria's question.

At last it was time for dessert. "My mother dropped off a cake," I told Billy, as we all ordered ice cream. Buck, Lizzie, and I got ours with chocolate sauce. Victoria wanted a strawberry parfait.

When Billy returned, everyone in the room turned to watch. For he was wheeling a huge, round birthday cake with thirteen candles along the sides and a Fourth of July sparkler in the center shooting off bright, sizzling sparks in all directions.

He set it down in front of me, and he and all the other waiters and waitresses gathered around our table and began singing. I looked around and thought I might burst with happiness.

"Happy birthday to you" — I could barely hear Roger singing — "Happy birthday to you" — and Buck, I think, was just mouthing the words. "Happy birthday, dear Gina" — Lizzie's voice was clear and sweet — *"Happy birthday to you!"* The loudest voice of all, drowning out even the waiters' and waitresses', was Victoria Chubb's.

The singing stopped and I stared for a moment at the cake. Then I took a deep breath and blew out all thirteen candles and the sparkler. Everyone clapped and Lizzie said, "This was a great party, Gina. It was a perfect idea. I can't believe you thought of it." Buck and Roger nodded.

"And it's a perfect way to end the Creative Social Studies Project," Victoria said. "I can't believe *I* thought of that."

Hearing her say that, my annoyance at Victoria returned. I remembered what I'd read in her report. I looked her straight in the eye. "So when do we get to read your report?" I asked her.

"What report?" she asked uneasily. Her eyes did not meet mine.

"The one you have to write for Mr. Dale about all of us," I said. "For the Creative Social Studies Project."

"Oh, *that* report," Victoria said. "It's not quite done yet. I have to make a few changes."

"In the word *team* there is no *I*," I said. "Maybe you could change it so it said that. After all, *all* of us working together is what made the project a success."

"I'll mention it," she said uncomfortably. For a second, she looked a little embarrassed. I suppose she was wondering if I had told the others what she had written.

Finally Buck broke the tension. "Forget about school," he said. "Let's cut the cake. And make my piece a big one."

"Right," Roger said. "Let's not think about school. Let's think about food. I want a big piece, too."

I knew he was right. Now was not the time to worry about school. So I took the knife and cut Victoria the first piece, a thick one with a yellow rose on it. As I handed it over to her she smiled gratefully, and I got the feeling there were still a lot of things about her I hadn't figured out yet. But right then, with all my best friends waiting for a piece of cake, I decided it really didn't matter. I was only thirteen. I had a lot of years left to try and figure out Victoria Chubb.